DESTINY

JUNCTION

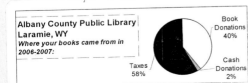

DESTINY
JUNCTION

Michael Phillips

Destiny Image Fiction
An Imprint of
Destiny Image® Publishers, Inc.
P.O. Box 310
Shippensburg, PA 17257-0310

ISBN 0-7684-2062-8

For Worldwide Distribution
Printed in the U.S.A.

This book and all other Destiny Image, Revival Press, MercyPlace, Fresh Bread, Destiny Image Fiction, and Treasure House books are available at Christian bookstores and distributors worldwide.

For a U.S. bookstore nearest you, call **1-800-722-6774**.
For more information on foreign distributors, call **717-532-3040**.
Or reach us on the Internet:
www.destinyimage.com

For God so loved the world that He gave His one and only Son, that whoever believes in Him shall not perish but have eternal life.

—John 3:16

A Foreword From the Author

This is not a flashy book. It is not a thriller. It is not a whodunit. It is not a romance. It is not a historical novel.

Its plot is not an exciting page turner. There are no mysteries, no hidden treasures, no rags-to-riches drama, no villains, no heroes.

Its characters are not scripted for Hollywood. They are ordinary people. I have not attempted to create artificial circumstances that end in perfect romances and happy solutions to every problem. Perhaps more than any other book I have written to date, I have tried here to portray life as it really is...but then, too, as I believe it can be depending on the choices we make.

Some may perhaps call that "life as it can be" idealistic. I hope others will see it as an exciting potential reality.

Though with different names and perhaps different professions, some of the characters you will recognize as people you know. You may even find yourself in these pages. Most of those whom you will meet are based in some way on real men and women and young people whose paths have crossed my own.

And you'll find me here too. I'm also one of the characters.

This is a story about life. What life means...and what it ought to mean.

One

6:43 A.M.

As the gray of an October morning gradually brightened, a sixteen-year-old boy, slender and pale, pimples on his face and the anger of loneliness in his eyes, walked hurriedly over the river. He clutched tightly at his overcoat. Not because of the cold, but to conceal what was hidden beneath it.

He glanced down at the water surging beneath him. There had been times he had thought of jumping from this spot and ending it that way. But whatever they said about drowning being peaceful, it gave him the creeps.

He had decided instead to go out in a blaze of glory...and take half the school with him.

The sound of an engine interrupted his thoughts. He looked behind him. It was a police car, moving slowly, heading toward him across the bridge.

His first impulse was to run. But that would be stupid. They'd bust him for sure, search him, and that would be it.

The car came closer, then drew alongside.

"You're out early, son," said a voice.

He glanced over at the cop through the open window of the patrol car.

"Yeah," he replied, "morning walk, you know."

"Saw you looking over the bridge back there...not thinking of doing something rash are you, son?"

"Heck no…I'm just out for a walk."

"Where do you live?"

"Over there."

Officer Sweet followed the direction of the boy's nod toward a cluster of houses on the other side of the river.

"All right, then…you'll be in school today?"

"Yeah, I'll be in school."

"Have a good one, then."

"Yeah, sure…whatever you say."

The car accelerated ahead, while the boy muttered a few inaudible profanities after it.

He continued on, reaching the other side and turning into the subdivision where he lived a dreary existence with his mother and sister.

He thought nothing of the houses as he passed them, did not think about the people who lived in them, nor pause to realize that most of them battled against their own invisible demons of silent pain just like he did.

Inside a corner house the boy passed as he made his way home, a woman had risen early.

She now sat with a Bible open on her lap, though her thoughts had drifted from the text. Barbara Kingston, active church member and women's Bible study leader, had prayed faithfully for her husband for years. But for some reason an urgency had built within her recently.

There was no doubt he had been different for the past month or two. She could tell something was on his mind. She could only hope it was the Lord.

"*Oh, God,*" she sighed, "*people need You so desperately, my Tom most of all. Turn his heart toward You, and give me the right words when the time comes.*"

In a fourplex down the street, a twenty-nine-year-old woman reached sleepily for her alarm clock.

Just about every morning at this time, Tracey Keane wondered if it was worth it. What kind of a life was this anyway, working in a lousy dead-end job for fifty cents above minimum? She hadn't gone to college to ring up Cokes, candy bars, and potato chips.

No, it wasn't much of a life. But what could she do? Her folks were both dead. Her older sister was in San Francisco, and they hardly ever talked. Tracey had no money, no prospects and hardly a single meaningful friendship. Most everybody her age, including her friends from high school, had married by now.

The fact that she was still a virgin did not cause her to feel good about herself, but rather was one more indication of the futility of her existence. What should have been one of her most priceless possessions, her purity, was for Tracey Keane a noose of failure around her neck. Nobody wanted her. She didn't *matter* to another soul on the face of the earth.

If she died and disappeared from the planet, who would care? Would her sister even bother to look into it? She hadn't had a date in two years. She wasn't good-looking and knew it. The gradual passage of years wasn't doing anything to help. How could you meet quality guys in a corner market that catered to a college lunch crowd that was younger and more immature every day? Where she spent her time, she encountered more skateboarders than potential relationships.

When it came right down to it, life was not just boring, it was drab and meaningless.

Tracey sighed and threw back the blankets. Tedious or not, what could she do about it? Rent was due tomorrow, and she had to pay her bills.

That meant she had to get up and go to work.

Two mothers with the same name made plans for the day. But how very different were their thoughts.

Annette Gonzales trembled inwardly, trying to hold back her tears, at what news the day might bring. She had to take her husband into the city for a biopsy. Suddenly it seemed their dream of a long and happy life was about to be taken away when it had only just begun.

She didn't know what to tell the children. How could they possibly understand what dread was caused by the mere sound of the word *cancer*?

At the same time, pastor's wife Anne Jefferson was in a gay and happy mood and had started work early on the special dinner she had planned for this evening.

It had always been her dream to have many children, at least three, maybe five or six. But after the birth of their daughter and the complications that had set in, the doctor made it clear that another pregnancy was not worth the risk.

Anne was too young for a hysterectomy. Harlowe was only a few years out of seminary. She had grieved at first. But as the years passed she came to realize that in some wonderful way God had poured the blessing of *ten* children into their one precious child.

Lynne was God's special angel to bless their first pastorate. As she grew, both the young pastor and his wife could not but be reminded of Luke 2:52, for surely their girl was growing in wisdom and stature just like the Lord.

Anne smiled to herself. And now their little girl was a woman about to embark on her own life's adventure. Lynne had told her that she would have to wait for the big news until tonight.

But Anne suspected well enough what her daughter and boyfriend had to tell them.

Two

TUESDAY, OCTOBER 14

9:57 P.M.

Tom remained in Barbara's thoughts all day.

The Kingstons had everything anyone could want—a nice home, a profitable construction business, three children doing well. They were a happy family in every respect...except one. When she and the children worshiped the Lord on Sunday mornings, the man who should be their spiritual head was most often either in his garden, fishing at the river, or in front of the television watching football. *She* was the women's group leader and music director. She was the one people in church called with their problems.

Tom was a fine man. She loved him no less than the day she married him. He was a considerate husband and good father, despite being gone many evenings consulting with clients or working on bids. But that came with his line of work. And he was highly respected in the community. There had been talk of his running for mayor.

Yet something would always be missing in their relationship until his spiritual condition was resolved. It had not always been this way. Tom's parents had helped build Destiny Junction Community Church. Some people still considered Tom and his brother Dave pillars of the church and spiritual giants as a result. Unfortunately, their wives knew better. Through the years the luster of popularity in the church had faded, and both were now barely on the fringes of church life.

Barbara rose, glanced at her watch, then went to the front window and looked out into the darkness. It was nearly ten. Why wasn't Tom home? He should have been back from his meeting in the city by now.

———◦◦◦———

Across town, another wife was also anxious for her husband's well-being. But her concerns were of a far more immediate nature than his standing with God.

Annette Gonzales sat nervously listening while her thirty-nine-year-old husband of sixteen years nodded and occasionally made a word or two of comment. She scanned his face for some sign of news, but his deadpan expression betrayed nothing. She knew the children were probably listening from their rooms, not fully understanding what was going on, but sensing enough from the events of the last few days to be worried. She had still not thought of a good way to tell them.

How could a single week so suddenly turn their lives upside down? But the day when Sam had discovered blood in his stool had changed everything.

At last the conversation seemed to be winding down.

"All right…yeah—I'll try," Sam was saying. "Thanks. Okay, sure—I'll see you tomorrow morning."

He hung up the phone and turned toward his wife. He drew in a long breath and let it out slowly.

"Well," he said, "that was Dr. Woo. I guess you figured."

Annette nodded, her eyes wide.

"She just found out the results. She knows the lab guy and got them after hours."

"And?" said Annette. She could hardly get the word out for the fear clutching her chest.

"It's like she thought—the biopsy was positive."

"Oh, Sam!" exclaimed his wife, her eyes filling with tears.

"She wants to see us tomorrow morning—to talk about our options."

———❖———

Three hours later, in a part of town not frequented at such hours by respectable people like Barbara Kingston and the Gonzales, a twenty-two-year-old single girl unlocked her hotel door and walked inside. It was dark and silent.

She began to undress—not for the first time that night, but thankfully it would be for the last—without turning on a light. A minute later she flipped the switch in the bathroom, started the water, tossed her scanty perfume-soaked clothes in a heap, and stepped into the shower.

She could not wash away what she had done—what she did every night. But it felt good at least to let the hot water pour over her at the end of the night's waking nightmare, and then go to bed, finally alone, her skin and hair and body clean again for a few brief hours.

Nothing could ever make her clean again on the inside.

She had lost the chance for that kind of cleansing by hopping a bus and taking it as far as the few bucks in her purse could get her. That wasn't far. She was less than a hundred miles from home. But she was worlds away from the life she had known such a short time ago.

She had grown up in a hurry. Now she was stuck here, trapped by the circumstances of her own making, with no way to go back…no way to be clean again.

———❖———

Another woman, older by fifteen years, battled a similar sexual demon, also knowing that true cleanliness of soul was forever beyond her grasp.

Sally Parker awoke in the darkness, sweating and panting in cold panic.

The dream had returned, the groping hands, the evil breath, the lecherous laugh…and the pain.

But it was no dream. It was far worse.

15

It was a memory…a living, horrible memory that kept returning, over and over in the black hours of night. Sometimes she lay awake, afraid to let herself go to sleep, knowing that when she did all the terrifying images would return. And with them the guilt.

How could she not feel shame? It took courage to face it. Maybe more courage than she possessed. She ought to talk to God about it. Obviously He knew of her past. But she struggled just as much with the question of whether He was there at all as she did with the nightmares.

Maybe she was afraid of what God would expect her to do.

Where could she go for help? To whom could she turn for answers?

She'd tried church. She'd been trying it for years. Right now she was sporadically attending *three* churches and counseling with *three* different pastors.

But if she didn't have the courage to talk to God, how could she talk openly to them? The responses they gave to her vague descriptions of her "problems" were all pat…formulas that sounded like they'd been looked up in some pastoral handbook.

Did pastors have anything to offer but platitudes? They didn't help *her*. How could they? Such men couldn't possibly understand!

It was hard to know where to go, or who to talk with about incest.

Not all homeless guys were bums and deadbeats, thought Bruce Penley as he crossed the street and sat down on the curb beneath the dim yellow streetlight and began munching on the leftover pizza he had just scored out of a dumpster at the back of Sergio's Italian Café.

He could work if he needed to. But why bother? This wasn't such a bad life. No responsibilities, no bills, plenty to eat if you knew where to look at the right time.

The boredom sometimes got to him. And the cold, he thought, clamping down on the end of pizza between his teeth, rubbing his hands together then stuffing them into the pockets of his ragged coat.

The fingers of his right hand fell upon something. Was it that half of a candy bar he'd found this morning—?

Nope...now he remembered...he'd eaten that for lunch.

Clutching whatever it was, he pulled the object out.

He looked down to see in his hand the small Bible that girl had given him this morning at the rescue mission. He'd forgotten about it.

He turned it over a few times, then started to toss it into the street.

At the last instant he hesitated.

He glanced at the small book again, now taking the piece of cold pizza in his left hand and slowly chewing at it.

Why not, Penley said to himself. Maybe he ought to read it. He'd promised his mother the last time he'd seen her—how long had it been, five or six years?—that he'd go to church.

Maybe this would do just as well. A little religion never hurt anyone, he supposed, though *he* didn't need it.

Besides, he had plenty of time on his hands and nothing else to do.

Anne Jefferson lay awake thinking happily of the events of the evening just past. Their only child had announced her engagement at dinner.

How quickly the years had flown by, thought the minister's wife. Lynne had given her heart to Jesus at eleven. Her own father proudly baptized her. And she had grown ever since in ways beyond her tender years. Perhaps her mother's heart was biased, but never, Anne thought, had she seen a young person so dedicated to the Lord as their own daughter. Always a happy smile, always a helping hand. What parent wouldn't be proud?

Lynne enriched their ministry in so many ways. After the Jeffersons had moved here to take the pulpit of Destiny Junction Community Church during Lynne's junior year of high school, some of the people in the church jokingly said that they were getting two preachers for the price of one.

Perhaps they had not been so far wrong, thought Anne with a fond smile. By the end of that same school year, a mini-revival was underway at the high school as a result of her daughter's influence—Bible studies during lunch hour, Christian students gathering to pray every day before class, dozens of the most popular girls and guys attending youth group at their church.

Even now, the high school Bible club was still active eight years after Lynne had helped start it. And she continued to have the same sort of impact on people wherever she went.

If having such a daughter meant not having *other* children to raise, then surely it had been worth it, thought Anne as she turned over in bed. God had answered her prayers, only differently than she had anticipated. She only had one *physical* daughter, but through her she had dozens, perhaps even hundreds, of *spiritual* grandchildren.

And after tonight's marriage announcement, she and Harlowe could look forward to grandchildren of the traditional variety as well!

Lynne was twenty-five...what a wonderful life she had ahead of her.

Three

Doug Taggart sat down in his first class seat and smiled to himself.

He had been working on this merger for seven months. Next week, after arriving home, the announcement would be made. Stock prices should immediately jump 30 percent.

The trip to New York had been more successful than he dared imagine. The small local bank that he and a handful of Destiny Junction's leading citizens had opened nine years ago on a million dollar shoestring would soon be listed on the NYSE. After a hundred years of an undistinguished history, the community was quickly growing past its sleepy frontier roots to become a thriving modern town. It was still small, but things were happening, thought Taggart. Someday this place would become a city. When it did, real estate prices would soar, and his own personal portfolio with them. And once the buyout he had just consummated was complete, with assets in excess of $525 million, and with earnings soaring, the bank's stock could double again in the next twelve months.

The thing had taken off more rapidly than any of the founders had foreseen. It was far and away the greatest business success story in Destiny Junction history. It had made him, and a lot of other men and women, wealthy beyond their dreams.

And, he had every reason to believe, if he played his cards right, this was only the beginning.

———————⋙◦◦◦⋘———————

As the banker sat back in his seat and contemplated the bright future ahead of him, in the town to which he was bound businesswoman Jeanne Carter glanced up from her desk. A young lady was bounding toward her with a bubbly smile on her face. The owner of the store rose and walked out of the office to greet her first customer of the day.

"Good morning, Lynne!" she said.

"Hi, Mrs. Carter."

"I heard Sean popped the question."

"Word travels fast!" laughed the young lady, flashing a wide smile. "Well, the rumor is true, I'm pleased to say. Sean talked to my father, then broke the news to me."

"Broke the news!" repeated Jeanne. "That's an odd way of describing a proposal of marriage!"

"I didn't mean it like that," laughed Lynne again.

"What did you say?"

"I accepted, of course!"

"We all had dinner together last night," Lynne continued. "You should have seen my mom."

"Happy?"

"Ecstatic!"

Jeanne laughed. She had already spoken with Anne, one of her best friends, this morning.

"When's the big day?"

"Not till a year from June—after Sean finishes seminary."

"Well, congratulations—I'm very happy for you. And your father?"

"Excited, of course. Daddy and Sean are already great friends. Natural-ly he couldn't be happier that my future husband is going into the ministry."

"How's that class at the college going you were telling me about?"

"I'm enjoying it," replied the pastor's daughter. "But the professor is such a skeptic. I can't imagine why she would want to teach a course in Celtic history. She gives the druids more importance than the ancient Christian priests. I'm praying for her, though I don't think she likes me very much."

"I thought everyone liked you, Lynne!"

"Hardly! Bubbly Christians rub some people the wrong way. And in this class, whenever I make a comment that is upsetting to the modern worldview, I know it irritates her. But somebody's got to speak up for the truth."

"And why not you, right? Are you still working down at the rescue mission?"

"I just came from there," answered Lynne. "We serve breakfast three days a week."

"Is Jim still there? I haven't seen him for a while."

"On and off. He worked with me this morning.—That reminds me...I need a Testament, Mrs. Carter, something inexpensive...there's a new man wandering around in Old Town. I gave away my last one to a sweet homeless man a couple of days ago."

Together the young evangelist and store owner walked toward the Bible alcove. Two or three minutes later they returned toward the center of the store, Lynne holding her selection. When she reached the counter she opened the Testament and began writing inside the cover.

"The Lord has really put it on my heart to pray for him," she said as she wrote. "This Bible is going to be his someday, though he doesn't know yet I exist."

"You're buying a Bible for someone you don't even know?"

"Not *yet*. But I will. I'm going to try to find him this afternoon."

"You're really something!" laughed Mrs. Carter.

"The day will come when he will read these words of mine and take them to heart," rejoined Lynne. "He doesn't know it yet, but he's going to give his heart to the Lord."

Jeanne laughed again.

"I wish I had your faith, Lynne!"

"You do, Mrs. Carter. This store is a ministry of faith. It is my favorite place to come in the whole town!" Lynne went on. "I know a lot of people feel that way. I share the Lord down at the mission, and at the college and the high school. You share the Lord through your store. People respond to the Lord in different ways, so we all have to do the work He gives us and then let Him take care of watering the seeds."

"You sound like Harlowe—do you give your sermon ideas to him?" asked the bookstore owner as the young lady paid for the Bible.

"My father's got plenty of his own," replied Lynne. "Gotta run or I'll be late for class. Thanks, Mrs. Carter. Lord bless you!"

"Good-bye, Lynne—see you next time."

Sam and Annette Gonzales sat soberly in the office of Dr. Sarah Woo listening to her outline the various options for Sam's cancer treatment.

It was all Annette could do to keep from breaking into tears. It was too awful. A week ago they had been making Thanksgiving plans. Now they were talking of surgery and radiation and chemotherapy.

Sam was only thirty-nine. He'd always been in good health, worked out three times a week, played basketball with his friends. They ate well and watched their weight. How could it have come upon them so suddenly!

They had no life insurance. If he couldn't keep working, what would happen to their health coverage? How long would the college keep him on? Groundskeepers were a dime a dozen. And what if—

Annette could hardly bring herself to think it.

And what of the children, their future, finances? She had never worked. How could they get by?

A thousand such terrible *what-ifs* had flooded her brain these last few days.

"...scheduled the surgery in the city for Friday, that's the day after tomorrow..." Dr. Woo's voice gradually intruded back into her hearing. "They will remove about three feet of your colon that was directly affected by the cancer. Then afterward, we'll begin alternating chemotherapy and radiation treatment on a six-week cycle. You'll have to go into Chambers for the treatments. I'm sure you know, Sam, that chemo can have unpleasant side effects, but we have every hope that..."

Again Annette's mind wandered. All she could think of was the children. What would she do if all this *didn't* work...and they were left alone?

A nondescript dark sedan pulled off the interstate and slowly made its way past the city limit sign into Destiny Junction.

This was the place. His next assignment.

The man at the wheel was nondescript as well, his face and receding brown hairline average, his clothes off the rack from K-Mart. Everything about his car, appearance and lifestyle were designed to blend in. He came, he went, without being seen, without calling attention to himself. In his line of work, to be noticed meant life, the chair or the chamber. He'd take out a contract on himself, no extra charge, before he let it come to that.

The only thing that might have distinguished the stranger in town, had one probed enough to notice, were his eyes. They were black and expressionless. Cold and hard. If the man had a soul, his eyes did not reveal it.

As he drove, he glanced to the right and left, looking for a motel. The cheap ones at the edge of town usually suited him just fine. Positioned for quick getaway. Nobody asking too many questions.

A sign caught his eye. "Adult Books and Novelties." A thin smile creased his lips. And there was a motel a couple hundred yards beyond it. That should do just fine. He'd be within walking distance of some cheap entertainment.

He slowed and pulled in.

In the trunk of his sedan lay two black suitcases, as nondescript as everything else about this visitor to the small town where many intersections of destiny were beginning to converge. One carried a few clothes and two or three disguises if he should need them. In the other were concealed the tools of his trade—a .380 caliber semiautomatic Ruger pistol with suppressor, and a three-piece 7.62 mm. Remington rifle he had had custom made in Chicago.

They could kill in a single shot. Both had done so many times.

———◆◆◆———

Harlowe Jefferson had never considered himself a particularly gifted man. He had come up through the ranks of the working class and had gotten through college and seminary the old-fashioned way—with hard work. He was not one of those pastors who wanted to write a book or preach on TV. Leave that to the showmen. Entertainment preachers, he called them.

His heart was for people. It always had been. It always would be. Common, ordinary, down-to-earth men and women.

Harlowe Jefferson *liked* people.

Maybe his daughter had gotten her love for people from him.

Whenever he sat down to think and pray about what message God wanted him to give next, the faces of his congregation rose in his mind. How could he help these people draw closer to God?

A hand-lettered plaque hung in his office. It hung there to keep him on track, to remind himself of life's bull's-eye, to readjust his priorities every day to the foundation of why he was in the ministry.

It read: *"People and practicality. They sum up the Lord's ministry…* make sure they do yours."

Practicality was his creed. He didn't care so much for hermeunetics, theology and obscure doctrines. He wanted to know how to *live* the Christian faith. He wanted to help his people do the same.

Harlowe Jefferson's perspective of the ministry was simple. *If Jesus said it, then we're supposed to obey it. How do we do so?*

Whenever someone came to him, for any problem—divorce, discouragement, financial difficulties, homosexuality, anger, bitterness, self-doubts—his approach was always the same: to open his Bible to the New Testament.

"Let's see what Jesus has to say," he would begin. "Then we'll see what you need to do."

To the mind of Harlowe Jefferson, the gospel was not complicated. It was straightforward enough. It told of a man's life—the man Christians called their master. It gave instructions about how they were to live.

As he sat in his study on this particular afternoon, his gaze drifted from the people and practicality plaque to the notepad on his desk beside his Bible. He had been thinking that it was time he confronted the people of his congregation with the urgency of the endtimes, and the clear choice facing men and women between two very distinct eternal destinies. He was no hellfire preacher, and he didn't intend to become one. Yet perhaps it was time to draw the distinction in unmistakable terms and make people face the fact that there were only two eternal options before them. Life was short, and they couldn't put off a decision forever.

Somehow he sensed eternity beckoning this town.

He knew many of those who listened to him every week probably weren't saved. It was time he laid the cards on the table in black and white. How could they live the Christian life if they had never given theirs hearts to the Lord?

"Lord," he whispered softly, "the time is short. What is in Your heart to say to the people of this community?"

Four

WEDNESDAY, OCTOBER 15

7:18 P.M.

Several blocks from the mission where the minister's daughter volunteered her time, in what might have been called the red-light district had the town been large enough, a girl named Heather stood before a mirror in a tiny hotel room, taking stock of the face staring out at her. She had had a decent night's sleep, considering, had lounged around most of the afternoon with nothing to do, and now it was time to get ready for another night of work.

It was an unusually pretty face, as she knew well enough. That had always been her trouble, enjoying the attention it brought her.

She wasn't enjoying it now, even though at the moment she was applying various colors to its features, almost as if she were painting a doll's face.

She hated it. But there was no escape.

She had been here a year surviving in the worst of possible ways. She could not quite bring herself to admit that she was a hooker. At first she had thought she wanted to hurt her father. Now she had shamed his very name. It didn't feel like she thought it would. What she had done made her sick.

But what did it matter now? Once begun, this was a road from which there was no turning back.

"Hey, babe," came the familiar voice through the door, "you ready?"

With one last wistful glance, avoiding her own eyes in the mirror, Heather turned with a sigh and left the bathroom. It was time to go to work.

———◆◦◦◦◆———

Sean Schaeffer and Lynne Jefferson were enjoying their first dinner out together since Sean's proposal.

The subject of their conversation, however, as was often the case, concerned spiritual things rather than their future, and had now drifted toward Lynne's history class at school.

"I'm uncertain what to do," she was saying. "I don't want to alienate them, but how long do you just sit and listen while everyone ridicules the Christian perspective? I don't want to be confrontational—"

"With your personality, Lynne," interjected Sean, "no one's going to think you're confrontational."

"You know what I mean. Sometimes you can have the best of intentions, but people still don't like outspoken Christians."

"That's their problem, not yours—as long as your heart's right, and you're speaking in love."

"I suppose, but—"

"This doesn't sound like my girl!" laughed Sean. "I've never heard you doubt speaking up for the Lord!"

Lynne smiled. But it was less than her characteristic wide, happy, optimistic smile.

"I guess I'm feeling a little beaten down," she said. "I just don't see *any* hopeful signs at the college. There are so few Christians, and most of them are afraid to say anything about their faith. The bias in every class is so modernistic. It doesn't seem like one tiny voice like mine makes any difference."

"You might not see all the ways God is at work," rejoined Sean. "You never know what's going on inside someone's heart. The Spirit is always busy."

"I know…you're right."

"And isn't that what our lives are all about?" Sean went on. "If I am planning to become a minister, I'm sure I will say things that will bother

28

people. Your father probably does too. It can't be helped. The gospel is a stumbling block to people with closed minds. But we can't stop speaking out. That's why I love the parable of the sower. Jesus says there are four kinds of people—some respond to the Word, others do not. Among those who do, there are different levels of response. The Word bears fruit in some lives, satan prevents it in others. Some people have depth of soil, others do not. But we can't know which people are which. As Christians we have to be faithful to sow spiritual seeds wherever we go. Sometimes those seeds are direct—words we actually speak. At other times they are indirect—acts of kindness we demonstrate to others. But we've got to keep sowing seeds."

"All right," smiled Lynne. "Message received. It's hard not to get discouraged when people misinterpret your motives and think you are pushy. But I will consider myself reinvigorated for the battle."

"Good for you."

"If the opportunity comes, I will speak up tomorrow—gently, of course! So, would you like to go to the high school on Friday to sow some gospel seeds with me there?"

"Sorry, I can't," replied Sean. "I have to get back to the city in the morning for a test in Dr. Fellowes' Church History class. I've missed too much school as it is commuting back and forth these last couple of weeks."

———————⋗∘∙∘∘∘⋖———————

Night club owner Vince Hackett looked up to see the dark imposing figure of Reggie Kincaid walking into his establishment flanked by two very different, though similarly dressed women. One of them was obviously well-experienced in her trade, the other was not.

Hackett felt sorry for the young kid. One look in her eyes and you could tell she'd gotten in too deep. But Reggie wasn't the kind of guy who'd let a girl change her mind without a fight. There were rumors, nothing substantiated, about some of the girls who had turned up missing over the years. He hoped the same didn't happen to this one.

His gaze drifted around the floor, pausing briefly at the stranger who had been here for an hour. He didn't like the fellow's look. He'd caught the man's eyes for an instant when delivering him a drink. A shiver had run up his spine.

Hackett's perusal of his clientele moved on to the guy in the corner booth, obviously waiting for someone. He looked out of place too, just like the kid at Reggie's side. He wondered what his story was.

Everyone had a story, thought Hackett. And most of the stories that turned up in this place were sad ones.

———◦◦◦———

Having no idea he was being scrutinized by the owner of the club, Tom Kingston sat in gloomy silence staring into his glass of Scotch.

He had never intended to allow it to go so far. He knew his wife had picked up on the fact that something was on his mind. He tried to hide it, but he'd seen the looks and glances. She knew him too well. He only hoped she hadn't figured out what it was.

But it wasn't so easy getting out.

Did he even want out? He wasn't sure.

The financial end of it was bad enough. He should never have listened to his foreman. The thing had had disaster written all over it right from the start...*a cousin who has a friend who's buying up development land next to...*

What an idiot not to have seen it coming! He should have just kept the money in the stock market. But he'd sold off most of their holdings and scraped together fifty grand, without Barbara's knowing, and plunked it into the scam, hoping to turn 200 percent within a year.

The only consolation was that his foreman had lost his shirt too.

Everything gone...the guy vanished without a trace. Fifty Gs down the toilet.

If word of it leaked out, his reputation in this town would be finished. He could forget his business, forget any more big contracts, forget being mayor.

Now he was trying to keep the company afloat with credit cards, hoping to low-bid enough jobs to keep his crew busy through the winter. But things were stretched too thin for comfort. He knew bankruptcy was looming. That was the trouble with expanding too fast. You were always on the financial edge. He'd taken on eight new men within the last year, and the payroll was eating him alive. If he could just land that government contract in the city, and shave costs here and there...he might be able to work his way out of this next summer.

The only bright spot in it all was meeting Michelle, who was handling the bids for the new office complex in Chambers. They'd hit it off from the first day he'd gone into the city to find out about the job. He'd asked her out to dinner since he was staying over, and...well, after that one thing led to another.

Even with the guilt that came with it, and the hassle of having to cover his tracks, he hadn't felt so alive in years. Michelle did things for him that Barbara could never even imagine. It was hard being the husband of a woman who was married to church first and him second.

Later that same night, while many customers were still enjoying the drinks served up in Hackett's establishment, in the city of Chambers a hundred miles away a man who had never been to such a place in his life woke suddenly. It was dark.

He glanced at the clock on the headboard. Two-eleven.

Without disturbing his wife, he quietly rose, put on his robe, walked into the darkened living room and sat down in his favorite chair.

Would he ever sleep through the night again without waking with reminders of the shattered dream? Nothing seemed to matter now—not his classes, not the seminary, not his reputation, not the book deal he was negotiating. He would trade it all in an instant to have their youngest daughter back.

The words that were ever present drifted unbidden through his brain for the thousandth time.

"I hate your life, your faith, your God…and I hate you. I'm leaving for good. I hope I never see you again!"

All the hopes of twenty years of parenting shattered in an instant. They had had such fun together as a family. He and Judith had been caring and considerate parents. They had taught their two children in the ways of God. And for what? For one of them to leave angry, rejecting God, yelling that she never wanted to set foot in their house again? He encountered broken families all the time—half his students came from them. But he had never expected his *own* to become a statistic pointing toward the breakdown of family life in the church.

They had not seen their daughter in a year.

Unconsciously the seminary professor opened the familiar devotional on the table beside him, paying no attention to the date. He began reading where the pages fell open.

"Sorrow came to you yesterday, and emptied your home. Your first impulse now is to give up, and sit down in despair amid the wrecks of your hopes. But you dare not do it. You are in the line of battle, and the crisis is at hand. To falter a moment would be to imperil some holy interest. Other lives would be harmed by your pausing…You must not linger even to indulge your grief."

Even before he had completed the paragraph, his eyes flooded with tears.

Slowly he set the *Streams* aside and slipped to his knees beside his chair.

"I know I haven't lived my faith much since that horrible day a year ago," he whispered. "I am sorry, Lord. It was like a freight train slamming into me. But I have been guilty of giving in to my despair. I just haven't been able to pick myself up. I am sorry. Forgive my weakness."

He paused and let out a long sigh.

"Wherever she is, Lord," he went on, "I pray that You would send people and circumstances to reach out and touch her spirit. Remind her of what she had here. Remind her of her training. I pray for the town or city where she is living, wherever it is. May Your Spirit come to life there, Lord. Descend upon it with Your salvation, not only for our daughter, but for all the people with whom she is in contact."

He sat for another twenty or thirty minutes in the darkness, then rose and returned to bed. He heard his wife stir.

"Matthew...what is it?" she mumbled.

"Nothing, dear. I just couldn't sleep."

"Is anything the matter?"

"No...just the usual. I was thinking about—"

His voice choked.

"I know," she replied, reaching out a tender hand as he lay down beside her.

"I...I just had to pray for her again. There's nothing else to do but pray."

"This isn't the end, Matthew," said Judith. "We cannot lose heart. We trained her up in the way she should go. We must keep believing that the Lord will be faithful, and that she will return to it in the end."

Five

Destiny Junction was not a large town. It had only two schools beyond the elementary grades, its one high school and the state college that had been there nearly as long as the town itself. On this day, personal and private dramas were unfolding that would ultimately impact both schools in very unexpected ways.

Early Friday morning, high school junior Trent Tolek took a small metal cylinder from its hiding place in his room, wrapped it up in his gym shorts, and stuffed the wad into his backpack. Security at the school was so lax, he didn't know why he bothered. He could probably sneak the thing in whole without anyone finding out. But this was his plan, so he'd stick to it. It would make the story good, and he would make sure people knew every detail. He was already writing it down for posterity—his reasons, the outline of his plan, how easily he had obtained everything. The minute it was over, his diary would show up all over the Internet. That's what would make him more famous than all the others. The whole world would read his story.

He had been at the high school two full years. This was his third. The highest grade ever to appear on his report card were the Bs he got in P.E. Beyond that there were only a handful of Cs. School was not his thing. He had finally figured that out. If he was going to make a name for himself, it would have to be from something other than school. He didn't have a single friend. His folks had split up two years ago. He had never done anything he was proud of. His mom was always on his case. He'd tried to get a job but couldn't. Nobody wanted to hire a pimply sixteen-year-old.

The whole world could go to heck as far as he cared. And maybe he'd just be the one to send it there.

He didn't really want to hurt his sister, even if she was a nerd. He'd have to figure some way to keep her from going to school that day. Slip her something in her juice to give her a stomachache. She was always getting sick anyway. Girls were weird that way, always complaining about headaches and stomachaches. She'd never know the difference.

He grabbed a handful of pills from behind one of several stacks of militia magazines and weapons catalogs, popped one in his mouth, pocketed the rest, then headed for the door.

⸻

Several hours later in a classroom at Northwestern State College, the discussion comparing the relative influence of druids and priests in northern Britain had grown lively. A hand went up from the class.

"Excuse me, Ms. Laudine," said its owner.

"Yes, Miss Jefferson—what is it?" asked the historian standing at the front of the class.

"I'm not sure you can dismiss the legitimacy of St. Columba's miracle," said the pastor's daughter, trying to keep her voice soft, "just because the account of it is described with flowery imagery."

"You're not saying you think the account is factual?" rejoined the instructor.

"I don't know," replied Lynne. "You give credibility to the druids. Why are you so biased against Columba just because he was a Christian priest?"

"Really, Miss Jefferson," rejoined the feminist professor, "are you implying that I am not an objective historian?"

"I mean no disrespect, Ms. Laudine. You know more about the Celts than any of us. But I'm sure you realize yourself that you are prejudiced against anything that gives a hint of a Christian interpretation."

"On what do you base that statement?"

"Because you always take the anti-Christian position. I simply don't think it is objective to automatically assume falsehood without asking if perhaps the hagiographical accounts of this period, though exaggerated, could yet be based on factual tradition. Isn't it something the historian is obligated to look at? But you instantly explain away every Columban miracle account."

"Come on," now added another student sarcastically, "you don't actually believe any of that, do you? Rocks floating on water—give me a break."

"I'm just trying to get you all to honestly face your anti-Christian bias," said Lynne, glancing at the speaker, then back to the professor. "It's just the same as I find in my Contemporary American Politics class. If a liberal Christian or Catholic or a Jew makes reference to his religion, it's seen as tolerant and broad-minded and as an *asset* to his politics. But if an evangelical makes the slightest comment about his faith, he is instantly lambasted by those who say he should keep his beliefs *out* of politics. The bias is obvious, but no one seems to notice."

"The situations are hardly the same," rejoined the instructor, nettled at having her objectivity called into question.

"You're right, of course, Ms. Laudine," replied Lynne. "I didn't mean to draw an exact parallel. All I am saying is that we have to look at these accounts we've been discussing and ask where they came from. I don't think we can assume them to be pure fiction."

"The next thing we know," rejoined Laudine, giving in to her annoyance and injecting her tone with unmistakable ridicule, "you'll be telling us that a man named Jonah *actually* lived for three days in a whale, and a snake *actually* spoke to a cave woman named Eve!"

37

"I *would* say so," replied Lynne calmly. "I believe the Bible is histori-cally true."

Most of the class snickered.

"Give us another break!" said the nineteen-year-old nose-ringed boy who had spoken earlier. "Get with the new century, Jefferson. I mean, get with the new millennium!"

The professor finally gave in and laughed outright.

"If you want to live in a fairy-tale world, Miss Jefferson," she said, "I don't suppose there is much I can do to stop you. But we have digressed long enough. I want to turn our attention now to the druids of Wales, and try to assess their impact in the development of middle ages Britain at this same time period."

Lynne Jefferson said nothing more for the remainder of the hour. Nei-ther students nor professor spoke to her as she left. The young man who had derided her walked down the corridor with several of his friends, joking and laughing at the idea that anyone today actually believed that the Bible was literally true.

Lynne left campus, stopped briefly at the market across the street to pick up something for lunch, where she spoke briefly with the checkout clerk, then walked to her car and drove to the high school.

As she went, a pair of eyes followed her. Then their owner slowly walked to his own car, an uncomfortable feeling gnawing at him in the pit of his stomach.

Part-time student and television cameraman Lane Rakestraw felt bad for the girl. Especially since he knew he should have said something in her defense. Everyone had laughed and snickered. But Lynne Jefferson was right about the bias. He had already noticed Professor Laudine's anti-Christian slant.

Why had he been afraid to speak up?

He had always more or less considered himself a Christian. But who would know it? Since moving here he hadn't gotten involved in a church. And when had he ever said or done one single thing because of anything he believed? Come to think of it...did he *really* believe at all?

He had always tried to tell himself that he just kept his belief to himself. But if he didn't have the courage to stand up for anything when it counted, how deep did his belief really go?

Rakestraw got into his car and tried to push the incident out of his mind. He'd think about it later. Right now he had to get to the station.

———— ⦿ ————

Across town at Destiny Junction High, sophomore Lidia Tolek took one last depressing look in the mirror, sighed, and prepared to face the most awful time of her day—lunch period.

She went through the same thing every day, coming into the bathroom, getting safely inside a stall, then pulling out her pocket mirror and stick of *ClearSkin* to see what she could do with her face for the second half of the day. Every time she looked in the mirror she hated what she saw—pimples, big nose, oily hair, glasses—dreading the thought of eating alone, trying to pretend she wasn't listening, keeping her head down so she wouldn't see the stares, the chuckles, the winks.

But there was no way to escape. Every day was torment. The glances her way, the overheard jokes from junior and senior boys. Being a geek and being fat wasn't the worst of it, it was being called both to her face.

It had been stupid, but secretly she had hoped someone might ask her to tonight's homecoming dance. Why did she even let herself think such things?

———— ⦿ ————

While Lidia sat on the closed toilet seat trying to disguise a new bright red pimple on her face, the door opened and she heard more girls come in. The instant Lidia recognized the voices, she froze. She would absolutely *die* if any of them found out she was there!

"What are you and Brock going to do *after* the dance?" one voice was saying.

"I don't know," answered another. "Maybe that depends on who gets king and queen."

"Don't be be a nit, Yvonne. You and Brock will get it for sure. I mean, get real."

Homecoming queen hopeful Yvonne Seymour checked herself out in the mirror as she listened to her friend, then flashed a seductive grin that she would try on Brock in another minute or two.

She had dreamed of this day, and this night, for years. After tonight's big football game, if everything went as she hoped, everyone would be looking at her—the most popular girl in the whole school.

"Maybe you're right," she said teasingly. "With this face, how could they pick anyone else! Come on, let's go."

———◈◇◈———

Down the hall from the girls' bathroom, Lidia's troubled brother— older by a year—surveyed the lunch crowd with sinister intent. All the football players in their game jerseys...the cheerleaders and song queens prancing around in their short skirts...everybody talking about the parade after school, then the game and dance.

He hated every one of these kids, the Yvonne Seymours and Brock Yates most of all.

He hated homecoming. He hated life.

If he had been ready, today would have been the perfect day. Let them all die in their uniforms! But he wasn't quite ready. So he would let them have their celebration. Then he would take them all out. It would make Columbine look like child's play. He would be more famous than Timothy McVeigh.

He'd been planning this all summer, and smuggling in parts of the gun in tiny pieces since the first day of school. He had some pieces in his school locker, some in his gym locker, and a few stashed in hiding places no one could guess. The most critical pieces—the ammunition and the trigger mechanism—he wouldn't bring until the last day. Even a locker search wouldn't turn up enough to give him away. There hadn't even been a locker search in over a year.

No one was worried. No one thought it could happen *here*. This was just a nice friendly little town.

Ha! thought Trent. It had never been friendly to him! When had any-one ever paid the slightest attention to what *he* was thinking or feeling?

Well, they would now!

Once everything was set, he just had to pick the moment.

The thought of actually dying himself hadn't altogether registered in his brain. It was the one loose end he still had to deal with. But once the cops were here, they'd take care of that end of it.

Having no idea of the plot against the school being hatched in the brain of her brother, when the coast was clear, timidly Lidia crept out of the stall, glanced at herself one last time in the large mirror over the sinks, brushed hopelessly once or twice at her hair, and left the bathroom. She would try to find someplace alone to eat her sack lunch.

Ahead she saw Yvonne Seymour and Jill Chin talking to a girl she didn't recognize. Lidia slowed until they were through, then continued on, glancing down as she tried to walk past the older girl.

"Hi," said the girl.

Lidia looked up hesitantly, thinking she must be talking to someone else.

"Hi," repeated the girl, smiling at Lidia as she went by, then took a few steps beside her to catch up. "I'm Lynne Jefferson. You doing anything for lunch?"

"Uh...I was just," began Lidia nervously, not knowing why this girl was talking to her. "No...I guess not."

"Would you like to come to Bible Club?"

"Why are you asking me?"

"I don't know," replied Lynne brightly. "You look like someone I thought might enjoy it. You see, I graduated a few years ago, and I come back every chance I get to tell girls and guys about what God has done in my life."

"Are those other two girls you were just talking to…are they going?"

"No, they weren't interested," answered Lynne. "The blonde girl just laughed when I mentioned the Bible Club. So what do you think?" she added with a friendly smile. "Would you like to join me? We'll have fun."

Lidia couldn't remember the last time anyone had actually been nice to her around here. For some reason, this girl almost—she could hardly imagine such a thing!—seemed to like her.

"Uh…okay," she replied. "I guess I will."

As they continued walking together, Lidia nodded slightly as a boy passed them. Lynne noticed the gesture.

"Someone you know?" she asked.

"My brother," answered Lidia.

"Do you suppose he would like to come too?" asked Lynne.

"No way," replied Lidia. "He hates religious people. He hates everything."

"That's sad. He must be very lonely."

"He's weird."

"Maybe so," smiled Lynne. "But I'll still pray for him. What's his name?"

"Trent. But believe me, you're wasting your time. God's the last thing he'd be interested in."

<hr />

An hour later Lynne left the high school and walked along the sidewalk to her car three blocks away.

Ahead she saw a lady, probably about seventy, walking with a slight limp with her right hand clutching a white cane, while two plastic bags, nearly full, dangled from her left. By the look of it, she had just come from the Safeway across the street. Lynne hurried ahead.

"Those bags look heavy," she said cheerily as she drew alongside. "Why don't you let me carry them for you?"

Startled, the woman glanced over. At first she didn't seem to understand.

"Oh…uh, that's all right," she said after a second or two. "I'll manage."

"I don't mind, really," insisted Lynne. "We seem to be going the same way anyway…my name's Lynne Jefferson." As she spoke, Lynne gently eased the bags out of the woman's hand.

"Well, all right," replied the lady, managing a smile. "Actually, it was a little heavy. I bought more than I intended."

"Then the Lord must be watching out for you. It seems He sent me along just at the right time."

"I don't know about that," laughed the woman. "I've never been in the habit of thinking that He pays much attention to me."

"Oh, but He does," rejoined Lynne as they walked along together. "You may not know it, but He is watching over you every minute."

"And why would He do that?"

"Because He loves you, of course," replied Lynne. "That's exactly what I told a dear lonely girl back at the high school just a few minutes ago—that she was very special to God. So are you. That's the kind of God He is—He loves us all."

"Well, Lynne," said the woman, "you've restored my faith in young people, whatever else you may say. My name is Margaret Sanderson."

"I'm pleased to meet you, Mrs. Sanderson—*is* it Mrs.?"

"Yes, but I'm widowed now. There's no one left for me now but my little dog."

"Oh, I'm sorry to hear that. Do you live nearby—can I give you a ride home? My car's not far."

"That's sweet of you, dear. I just live in those green apartments up ahead on the other side of the street."

"Then I'll walk the rest of the way with you."

Six

Saturday, October 18

6:58 A.M.

Having no idea that the high school's homecoming game and dance had been held the previous night, nor that at this very moment events were rapidly unfolding downtown that would turn this small college community upside down, Sally Parker came slowly awake and glanced out into the light of morning. It was always a relief when morning finally came and the nightmares could be forgotten for another day.

A brown leaf glided on an invisible breath of air past the window to the ground.

From her upstairs window she watched as several others slowly followed in lazy succession, drifting back and forth until they came to rest on the wet earth below.

A winged swoosh interrupted the sight. A moment later an impertinent rapping disturbed the morning tranquility. The watcher glanced higher into the near-naked branches of the oak. The red-crowned woodpecker had wasted no time and was now pecking energetically in search of its breakfast.

Sally smiled at the sight, then turned away, rose from her bed, and began to dress for the day.

The expression that gradually faded from her lips was an autumn smile—thin and sad. A smile without joy. The woodpecker and leaf had prompted what was *called* a smile…but they could not bring hope.

It was a depressing time of year. And it would only get worse. Winter was coming. These were months that made it all the more difficult to forget, when the pain bit deep and refused to leave. Especially when the dreams came.

Would the memories ever go away?

Sally knew the answer, though she would probably continue asking the question every day for the rest of her life. Of course they wouldn't go away. The silent, inner demons of guilt and accusation would torment her until death finally released her from them.

It would be a relief to die, she thought. To sleep forever where no dreams, no thoughts and no memories could get into her mind.

Across an empty field, where cows and sheep occasionally grazed but mostly thistles grew, the residents of a green and white apartment complex were still asleep at this early hour.

The town of Destiny Junction was not yet growing by any great leaps and bounds, but what growth there was had been coming east. The Redwoods was among several new clusters of apartments that had gone up in the last five years at the edge of town not far from the high school, where they still shared the open landscape with a few animals.

From an upstairs window an elderly woman sat in her chair looking absently out at the same oak across the field whose winged visitor and dying leaves had drawn the attention of Sally Parker.

Margaret Sanderson was not thinking of leaves or woodpeckers, however. Nor did she know that her neighbor's name was Sally. The season of her aloneness had come, and all she did was endure it.

Her mind drifted back to her encounter with the friendly young lady yesterday who had carried her grocery bag and walked her home.

Nothing like that had happened to her in years.

How could one moment of contact with another human being make such a difference? But it was a lonely world. The simple fact of the matter was that having another face to smile into and talk to *did* make a difference.

She had spent seventy-three of her seventy-six years in the city, enjoyed a decent marriage, raised a family, risen in her career, and now she was by herself, husband gone, working years past, her three children scattered across thousands of miles.

Why she had moved to Destiny Junction, where she didn't know a soul, was still a puzzle. When she tried to explain it, the words that came out of her mouth hardly made sense even to her. How could anyone possibly understand?

"I visited Destiny Junction once when I was seven," she had told the girl yesterday. "I always remembered that visit, and thought it a nice little place. So when my husband died, I decided to move here."

That was three years ago. In that time Margaret Sanderson hadn't made a single friend.

Until yesterday. Now she wondered if she might be fortunate enough to see the girl called Lynne again.

Charlie Sweet steered his patrol car left, glancing absently toward The Redwoods apartments as he passed and headed back toward town.

A quiet morning, he thought. Another hour to go on his shift, then back home and—

His tranquil thoughts were suddenly interrupted by a blaring call from dispatch over the radio.

"Car three...come in! Charlie, you there?!"

"Sgt. Sweet...yeah, I'm here."

"Where are you?"

"Out by the fairgrounds."

"Get downtown—I mean fast!"

Already the police car was squealing in a rapid arc and laying rubber behind it. "What's up?" said Sweet as he flipped on his siren and ground his foot to the floor.

"Don't know—it's still sketchy. We might have a homicide."

Seven

SATURDAY, OCTOBER 18

7:10 A.M.

The importunate beep of a pager suddenly interrupted the morning's tranquility in the living room of an expensively appointed home in the fashionable south side of Destiny Junction.

Local television newscaster Leslie Cahill glanced toward it, took another sip of her morning's coffee, contemplated for a moment ignoring it, then stretched across to the table and picked it up.

It was the station calling. It always was. At least they'd let her sleep today until 6:45 and enjoy a few sips from her cup. But her twenty minutes of peace was over.

"Leslie," said a voice on the other end when she called in, "we've got a breaking one...might be big."

"What's up?"

"There's been a shooting down in Old Town, by one of those cheap hotels on the waterfront."

"And?"

"Daughter of somebody in town, they said—I just picked it up on the scanner. No name, but the cops are all over the place. There's a manhunt going on for the shooter right now."

"How many people involved?"

"Don't know, but it just came on…get down there ASAP and see what you can find out."

Already Cahill was on her feet and moving toward her bedroom, knocking off her slippers as she went.

"I'm on my way. Get Rakestraw on it too in case I want to go on camera with something live for tonight."

Cahill switched off the phone, tossed it onto her bed, and began quickly fumbling through her closet for a dress.

Destiny Junction wasn't populated enough to have a huge Bible bookstore, but its Christian community was grateful for Jeanne Carter's reasonably-sized shop. Most small towns had to depend on mail order or the nearest city for Bibles, music, church supplies and other Christian products. But around here Christians did their shopping at The Answer Place.

It was the intangible feeling of the Spirit's presence that drew people even more than the books, cards and gifts, and it was the reason for the store's success these twenty-five years since Jeanne had begun it almost as a lark during her college days. Some of her best customers compared it to having a little church in the middle of the business district where anyone could go for a brief respite from the world.

When Jeanne's longtime acquaintance Jim Franklin walked in shortly after opening about 9:45 on that fateful Saturday morning, however, he wasn't thinking about the pleasant atmosphere. Jeanne knew instantly from his expression that whatever he had on his mind, it was serious.

"Did you hear about Lynne?" he asked somberly.

"No…Lynne who?" asked Jeanne.

"Jefferson," replied Jim. "She was shot a couple hours ago."

A sharp gasp of shock escaped Jeanne's mouth as her hand went to her mouth. She was afraid to ask what next came to her mind.

"Don't know much more," said Jim, shaking his head. "They took her to the hospital. I haven't heard anything more."

"Oh, Lord Jesus," Jeanne exclaimed, finding her voice the moment the tears began to flow. "Take care of the poor girl!...She was just in here day before yesterday."

"I know," Jim nodded.

"Let me know the minute you hear anything."

"I will—I'm on my way to the church now."

Eight

SATURDAY, OCTOBER 18

7:58 A.M.

Judith and Matthew Fellowes had just finished a quiet breakfast a hundred miles away in Chambers. Matthew rose, kissed his wife, then picked up his briefcase and headed for the door.

"I'll be at the seminary most of the morning," he said. "Sorry to ditch you on a Saturday, but I've got to try to finish up that chapter on the Reformation before next week. I ought to be back by one or two."

His wife accompanied him to the porch, watched him drive away a minute or two later, then turned back into the house. As she returned to the kitchen, the professor's wife absently glanced toward the small television her husband always turned on for the day's weather.

A special bulletin was just coming on.

Something serious had apparently just happened in one of the small towns up north.

Judith walked toward it to turn up the sound.

Catholic priest Father Lawford Kimble heard the news on the radio in the rectory following eight o'clock mass. The young marrieds group had a barbeque planned for tomorrow, and he was keeping an eye on the weather.

"...police are now combing the area," he heard as he walked into his study from the radio he had left on. "According to Deputy Chief of Police Jack Snow, every available unit has been called in and people are advised to keep away from Old Town. Stay tuned for further developments."

———◦∞◦———

Nineteen-year-old Richard Ray had been out for a walk early.

It was a year and a half since he'd left home. He'd used up all the money his dad had given him, and sometimes he just couldn't stand his cold dump of an apartment. Several times a week he went out to breakfast at the Junction Café. He couldn't afford much more than oatmeal and coffee, but at least it was warm and there were people around. And the lady behind the counter recognized him now. Any human contact felt good.

He knew his mother would freak if she saw him. He'd lost probably twenty pounds. Every once in a while she sent him a care package filled with cookies. If he went home he knew the first thing she would do would be throw her arms around him and fix him a huge meal.

But he just couldn't deal with it. Maybe later. He hadn't written to her in a year. It brought back too many memories.

As he opened the door of the café, the sound of a screaming siren came in with him.

"Morning, Dick—what was all that about?" rasped the blond behind the counter.

"Don't know," he replied, sitting down at the counter. "I been hearing cop cars for the last half hour."

"Yeah, come to think of it, so have I.—What'll it be?"

"Just give me a cup of coffee, Dixie," replied Richard, glancing outside again as another police car sped by.

———◦∞◦———

In a booth across the café, insurance agent Scott Peyton was engrossed in the morning's *Wall Street Journal*. After the second siren zoomed past he glanced up.

He downed the last of his coffee and rose.

He probably ought to find out what was going on. If it was a fire or robbery or anything involving property, there was a good chance one of his clients could be involved.

———◦◦◦———

Driving back from Chambers the morning after Sam's surgery, Annette Gonzales was in a somber mood. Her brain was still reeling from this sudden calamity that had slammed into their lives. She had just been thinking that it might be time to start going to church.

The song playing on the radio came to an end.

"A bulletin has just been received," the DJ's voice broke in, "of a shooting in the town of Destiny Junction north of Chambers—"

Jolted suddenly out of her gloomy reverie, the first thing to come into Annette's mind was the children. She had left the three with her sister.

She reached to the radio and turned up the sound.

———◦◦◦———

Down the same street about half a mile away from where Jim Franklin had first carried the news, another bookstore owner inserted the key into the lock of the front door and walked inside a run-down building on the outskirts of town. He didn't open till 10:30. Most of his customers kept night hours and slept mornings.

Rex Stone inched his way through the blackness to the light switch. There weren't many windows in this place. The ones there were had been boarded up. No free gawking at the merchandise.

He was lucky if Adult Books and Novelties grossed a hundred bucks a day. But he wasn't in it for the money. He got a thousand a month disability, and if he could make a profit of fifteen or twenty a day on top of that, fine with him.

It gave him something to do...and it fed the porno habit he'd had since youth.

He had been out late last night himself with some chick and slept till almost nine. He hadn't heard the sirens, nor had turned on radio or TV. Thus Rex Stone had no way of knowing what had happened a few hours earlier.

Behind him, footsteps echoed on the bare floor.

He turned. A man had just entered…the same guy who had been in two or three times in the last couple of days.

The customer nodded without expression.

"You're out early," said Stone.

"Yeah. Staying in the motel over there. Can't hardly sleep with all the noise. What are the cops and sirens all about?"

"Beats me. I just got here."

The man began absently to look around.

"You got business in town?" asked the store owner.

"You might say that," replied his customer without looking up.

"What kind?"

"The kind I keep to myself."

Rex Stone got the message. If the guy didn't want to talk, that was okay with him.

———◦◦◦———

Tom and Barbara Kingston had planned a family outing at the river for Saturday afternoon. There wouldn't be many more opportunities before winter. And clouds were moving this way. Rain could be falling by tomorrow.

"It's nice to have you with us for the day," Barbara was saying as they drove. "You have been so busy with appointments."

"Yeah," shrugged Tom, keeping his eyes on the road. "Busy time, you know." Even as he spoke, his mind was elsewhere. Yesterday he'd received a repossession letter for two of the new trucks he'd bought just before the investment fiasco. If he didn't come up with three back payments by next Friday, amounting to over $2,500, the trucks would be gone. He was afraid this was only the beginning.

"Would you like to go to church with us tomorrow morning?" said Barbara's voice interrupting his thoughts.

"I don't know..." said Tom noncomittally. "Maybe. I'll see how the day goes. Gotta go to the city on Tuesday."

"It is always nice when we go as a family," Barbara added.

Tom said nothing.

"Daddy, why don't you go to church with us?" came the voice of a six-year-old.

"Daddy is very busy, dear," said Barbara, turning to their youngest daughter in the back seat. "He comes when he can."

"My teacher at church says that people who don't go to church will go to hell."

The two older children on either side of her glanced over at one another. An awkward silence filled the car. Absently Tom reached for the radio. He didn't need this.

"Daddy, where is hell?" persisted the youngster. "Have you been there?"

"Barbara," Tom finally snapped, "get her to shut up!"

Nine

Word of the day's events spread through Destiny Junction like a brush-fire. By six o'clock that evening, every eye for miles was glued to a television set.

"This is Leslie Cahill, Channel 3 Eyewitness News," began the newswoman in her customarily serious tone. "The town of Destiny Junction has been reeling all day as news spread of the shocking murder early this morning of twenty-five-year-old Lynne Jefferson, well-known daughter of Community Church minister Harlowe Jefferson.

"Police were called to the scene in Old Town at approximately six-thirty-five by an anonymous female caller..."

***

In shock and horror, Tracey Keane gazed at the smiling image of Lynne Jefferson being shown on her television screen.

She knew that face!

It was the same girl who came into the market across from Northwestern State every several days, bright and friendly, always with a kind word and smile. She usually bought a Coke and a sandwich, or an apple or banana.

She had seen her just yesterday! And come to think of it—

59

Tracey jumped up from her chair and darted across the room where she had laid her purse. She fumbled to open it. A few seconds later she held the tiny crumpled wad of paper she had stuffed inside. Lynne Jefferson had given it to her when she checked her out at the register yesterday just a little before noon. She had talked to her just *yesterday*...and now she was dead.

Tracey returned to her chair, gently unfolding the paper, then sat down and began to read.

------◆◆◆------

As Cahill went on to describe the gruesome details, most of the membership of the church listened weeping in their homes.

All had heard, but no one wanted to believe it could be true. Now suddenly the awful finality of the stark word *murder* sent chills of renewed horror through the hearts of everyone who knew Lynne. Christians from every church in town mourned, for Anne and Harlowe Jefferson were two of the most widely respected individuals in Destiny Junction.

------◆◆◆------

Margaret Sanderson had listened to the noon television news in tears.

By now a photograph was being shown. She knew she would not again see the girl who had befriended her just yesterday.

She did nothing for the rest of the afternoon but sit in a stupor. That evening as the report came on again, she watched in continued shock. All at once, the loneliness of her life bit deeper than ever.

"Why, God...*why* did this have to happen!" she said softly, then at last broke down and wept for the girl she had known for only a few minutes.

------◆◆◆------

"A motive for the shooting has not yet been established," the newswoman was saying, "though a suspect, forty-two-year-old Hank Dolan, has been arrested and is now in the county jail awaiting arraignment. According to the police, Dolan arrived in Destiny Junction only last week and has reportedly been living on the streets during his brief stay."

Brock Yates had to admit the evening's news shook him.

But why? He didn't know the dead girl. But the instant they had flashed up her photograph, the weirdest sensation came over him that her eyes were still alive!

And that they were looking straight into him. It was so strange! He actually felt like she *knew* him.

She looked familiar, now that he thought about it. He turned away from the TV and tried to force the dead girl out of his mind.

Maybe that was it. She reminded him of Yvonne.

Yvonne—now there was a more pleasant subject! He hadn't been able to get *her* out of his mind ever since Friday's dance.

They were the toast of the night—she the homecoming queen, him the hero of the game…a 53-yard touchdown run with seconds left. Everyone had been ga-ga over them, and Yvonne's big green eyes were ga-ga over *him*.

Who could ask for more? College scholarships would start pouring in any time. He was the man at Destiny High, and everyone knew it.

Unconsciously Brock glanced back at the TV.

Why did the dead girl's eyes unsettle him so?

"Miss Jefferson," the telecast continued, "who has been involved with the ministry of the rescue mission on Second Street for several years, was canvasing the streets early this morning. According to Bruce Penley, who apparently spoke with her only moments before the shooting, Miss Jefferson was passing out leaflets and inviting people to the mission for breakfast."

The camera now broke to a scruffy homeless man who had been interviewed earlier in the day.

"She came by and was friendly and smiling like she always was," Penley said, glancing nervously toward the camera. "Don't know why anyone'd want to hurt a girl like that. She was always nice to the likes of us down here. She gave me a little Bible just a few days ago."

He pulled his hand out of his pocket and held the Testament up to the camera.

"She invited me to the mission this morning," he said, "and then I seen her go off down toward First Street, and I knew Dolan was down there 'cause I seen him drunk under a garbage bin last night. And I told her that she ought to maybe not go down there. And she paused for a bit and then turned and asked me why, and I said 'cause I'd seen Dolan down that way. I said that he was a bad one and he could be rough and that I didn't want nothing to happen to her. But she just smiled and said, 'Mr. Dolan needs the Lord just as much as you do, Mr. Penley. I'll see you at the mission!' "

Where he watched in his own motel room, Wolf Griswold silently cursed.

What rotten luck!

How could he kill the man if he was sitting in jail? Not only had he wasted the time driving here, he'd wasted two days in this dump setting the thing up. The hit was supposed to have gone down tonight. Now this!

Maybe he'd nose around and see what was up. If they moved Dolan, that might be his chance. He should probably contact his boss too, and make sure the hit was still on.

The interview with the homeless near-witness continued.

"I tried to stop her," Penley was saying. "But she turned and went off down toward First Street. She didn't seem afraid of nothing. Then it must have been five or ten minutes later, I heard cursing, and I knew it was

Dolan's voice, then shouting, something like, 'I don't need none of your religious charity!' or something like that, though I can't be sure. But it was Dolan all right. He sounded mighty mad. I stopped and listened for another minute, but it was quiet after that. Then the next thing I heard was the gunshot, and I figured something real bad had happened."

He looked away, wiping at his eyes. The camera broke off and returned to Leslie Cahill live in the studio.

———◦◦◦———

Remembering the lunch she'd spent with Lynne Jefferson only yesterday, Lidia Tolek watched the evening news in disbelief.

As soon as the story was over, she went to her room, lay down on her bed, and began to cry. Tears were not new to Lidia. She cried alone in her room almost every night. But this was the first time in a long while that she had cried for someone other than herself.

———◦◦◦———

"Miss Jefferson was apparently holding a small New Testament in her hand at the time of the shooting," newswoman Cahill continued with her report. "She was still clutching it tightly when she died en route to the hospital, one of her fingers between the pages of John's Gospel. When her mother and father came to identify the body, they were given the Testament, where, after removing it from her hand, the attending physician had placed a marker in the spot Miss Jefferson's finger had lain.

"Dr. Jefferson thanked Dr. Woo for her thoughtfulness, then smiled and was heard to remark, 'I am not surprised. This was Lynne's favorite passage. Her whole life was based on John 3:16.' "

———◦◦◦———

Yvonne Seymour was with her friend Jill Chin at the mall during the dinner hour. A few minutes after six they were walking by an electronics store where twenty silent televisions suddenly displayed the face of Lynne Jefferson to passersby.

"Hey, isn't that the girl that was at school yesterday?" said Yvonne, slowing her step.

Jill looked toward the store. A sudden fear seized her chest.

Slowly they went inside. The clerk was absorbed with someone else. The sound on one of the sets was turned on. They walked toward it.

When the two girls walked out of the store a few minutes later, both wore sober expressions. Neither said a word for several long minutes. Suddenly they were no longer in the mood for shopping.

———————◦◦◦◦——————

When Lidia left the living room, her brother Trent turned off the TV. He didn't want to hear about it. Who cared anyway? They were all going to die eventually, so what was the big deal? He went to his room and began rummaging around in one of several hiding places for his stash of pills. He was getting jittery and needed something to calm his nerves.

———————◦◦◦◦——————

Dr. Carole Laudine listened to the news in somber silence. Disturbing feelings of guilt stirred within her. The caustic remarks she had made in class yesterday replayed themselves over and over in her memory. She had always considered herself independent and self-sufficient. Pangs like this were not something she knew how to handle.

———————◦◦◦◦——————

The following morning everyone at Destiny Junction Community Church went through the motions of the worship service in stunned silence. The predicted storm had come during the night and a persistent rain fell all morning, blanketing Destiny Junction with a gloomy gray. Neither Pastor Jefferson nor his wife Anne made an appearance. The assistant pastor fumbled through with an attempted sermon on God's ways being higher than man's ways. But neither she nor the congregation felt comforted as a result.

After the service, nearly everyone stood around outside, not exactly knowing what to do yet not wanting to leave. The poor Jeffersons, everyone said. What they must be going through.

Ten

Aspiring newspaper journalist Bertie Snow knew that in a small town like Destiny Junction, the human interest angle was the ball game.

If he could get the inside scoop from Hank Dolan, his piece would not only be read by everyone in town, it also would have a good chance of being picked up by the *Chronicle* in the city. That could be his ticket out of this little hole in the wall and onto the staff of a major paper. A reporter paid by piece work could never make it around here.

It didn't hurt that his uncle was Deputy Chief of Police. That would buy him ten minutes with the guy. Then it would be up to him to see what he could do with it.

It was not without some quivering of his knees that he followed his father's burly brother down the row of cells. He had certainly not inherited their side of the family's physical attributes. Bertie knew well enough that if Dolan wanted to get rough, he could probably break his neck before anyone would be able to stop it. But this was the chance of a lifetime. He drew in a breath and tried to forget that the man was in jail for murder.

His uncle stopped and inserted a key into the lock of a cell to his right. Bertie drew alongside and looked in. A man who looked as mean as his reputation sat on the edge of the bed staring back at them.

"You got a visitor, Dolan," said the deputy.

67

"That little pipsqueak don't look like no lawyer."

"He isn't a lawyer."

"Then I don't want to see him."

"Please, Mr. Dolan, " began Snow, "if I could just have a minute or two of your time—"

"Yeah, right!" Dolan spat back. "You can see I'm a pretty busy man— I ain't sure I can fit you in," he added sarcastically. "What is it you want! I ain't interested in seeing nobody."

"I'm a reporter," replied Snow. "I wondered if you'd like to tell your side of the story."

Dolan shrugged. It was all the okay the policeman needed. He opened the cell door. Bertie walked in. Two seconds later the iron lock clanked shut behind him.

"I, uh…I understand Lynne Jefferson invited you to the rescue mission," Bertie began, standing awkwardly in the middle of the cell and taking out a small tablet.

"Yeah, she invited me," Dolan replied, a little more calmly. "She was always trying to strong-arm people to go to that lousy place."

"But you didn't want to go?"

"I had other plans."

"So you shot her for inviting you to breakfast?" asked Snow.

"I ain't saying I shot her," snapped Dolan.

"All right, then, just tell me why you got upset. You were heard yelling at her."

"Maybe I don't like do-gooders interfering in my life."

"How did she interfere?"

"She was always preaching at me. I just finally had enough of it, that's all. I didn't want her talking idiotic Bible trash to me. I didn't want to go to the mission. So I told her to leave me alone."

"Then what happened?"

"I turned and walked away."

"And then?"

"She just kept talking...talking away at my back. She wouldn't quit, wouldn't take no for an answer."

"What did she say?"

"Just a bunch of fool nonsense about Jesus loving me and that she was going to keep praying for me no matter what. I was mad by then. I mean she had no right to keep on like that when I'd told her to leave me alone. I mean, I got the right to be left alone, don't I?"

"What did you do?"

"I turned around and I walked back to her. I got up in her face, I don't mind telling you. I said, 'Look, little girl, I don't need none of your religion. I don't need your mission. And I don't want you praying for me, you hear me! So you just get out of here. I'm telling you, if you try to pray for me again, I'll—'"

He stopped, seeming to come to himself. "Well, never mind what I said," he added, then laid down on the bed.

"And," said Snow, "...did she pray for you, I mean, there on the street?"

"I said all I got to say," replied Dolan.

"Just answer me one more question. Was she carrying a little New Testament?"

"Yeah, she was always carrying it and reading stuff out of it. I never listened, but other folks down there did. I finally had enough of it."

———◦◦◦———

Heather Fellowes sat silently on the edge of her bed in her sleazy hotel room.

She couldn't get the memory of the shooting out of her mind...and the last words she'd heard out the window of her hotel room...words cut short by the explosion of gunfire that had ended the girl's life.

I pray right now...

Words of prayer so familiar. They could have been—

No, she couldn't go there. Remembering her past hurt more than the awful sound of the shooting.

Heather had hardly slept all last night, or today. She knew she had to tell someone. But who?

She didn't want to get involved with the cops. They would start asking too many questions.

But *someone* had to know.

———◆◇◆———

Leslie Cahill, from whom so many had first heard the news, wondered why the murder was having such an effect on her. She tried to concentrate on her other work, but to no avail. Most stories were just news stories, detached, impersonal. You had to keep an emotional distance in this business. You would go crazy if you let yourself get personally involved. But this one was different. She couldn't get the Penley interview out of her mind, and the sight of that New Testament he had held up in her face.

———◆◇◆———

Cameraman Lane Rakestraw from Channel 3 News got up Monday morning. Immediately the Jefferson murder flashed back into his mind. Without planning it, almost before he realized what he was doing, he found himself looking about his apartment for his old Bible. Why, he couldn't say. He hadn't cracked its pages in years. But somehow it seemed the right thing to do in the wake of what had happened.

He sat down with the book on his lap. He remembered the Christmas his mom had given him this Bible. He opened the cover and read the inscription: *To my dear son Lane, with all my love and prayers, Mother.* He knew his way around well enough from his training as a kid. He turned to the second book of the New Testament and began to read: "The beginning of the gospel about Jesus Christ, the Son of God..."

Meanwhile...banker Doug Taggart found himself unusually subdued all weekend. The girl's father had just been in to see him about a car loan and he had not been able to get the poor man out of his mind. Maybe he should postpone the announcement of the merger.

Patrolman Charlie Sweet could not stop the vision from recurring over and over of the girl lying there on the sidewalk, blood still warm oozing out of her chest onto the pavement. All night and all the next day it kept coming back. The image haunted him. He could almost see the hint of a smile still on her face.

Sally Parker's melancholy thoughts turned introspective when she heard the news. Was *she* ready to die, to face eternity? She didn't even know the girl, yet her death set off a series of questions within her that she didn't know how to answer.

Jim Franklin was not in church on Sunday, nor did he return to the rescue mission for days. No one knew where he was.

Richard Ray was thoughtful when his waitress friend next saw him. He recognized Lynne Jefferson. He had seen her around Old Town, where exactly he couldn't remember. Somehow the sight of her reminded him of home, and filled him with odd sensations of nostalgia and sadness.

Dixie Judd remembered Lynne too. The girl came into the café occasionally and had once given her a tract to read. She had called it her testimony, whatever that meant. She'd kind of like to read it now, Dixie thought. But that had probably been a year ago, and she'd thrown it away.

Dr. Sarah Woo, who had pronounced Lynne Jefferson dead at 7:33 on Saturday morning, grieved more than usual for the poor man and wife who had arrived at the hospital too late to see their daughter alive. She had known them for years, and knew how badly Anne had wanted children. Now her only daughter had been taken from her. It all seemed so harsh, unfair and wrong. How could God allow this to happen to such good people? How could such a terrible tragedy result in anything good?

Eleven

The Answer Place had been buzzing with people all morning. Everyone was talking about Lynne. An hour earlier Jeanne Carter had posted a notice for the memorial service.

The store was empty briefly a little after one when the reporter came through the door.

"Hello, my name is Bertie Snow," he said as he walked straight to the counter. "I work for the *Standard*. I am doing a story on last week's shooting. I understand you sold Lynne Jefferson the Bible she was holding when she was shot. I would like to know more about it."

Jeanne Carter tried to smile, though it was difficult to think of Lynne. She had just managed to stop crying a few minutes before the reporter came into the store.

"Yes," she nodded, drawing in a slow breath to steady herself. "I remember the day she bought her first Bible to give away. I doubt if she was more than fourteen or fifteen at the time. Since then she must have bought more than fifty Bibles or Testaments for those she was witnessing to."

"Witnessing, what does that mean?"

"Telling people about Jesus. That was Lynne's whole life."

"Why?" asked Snow.

"She believed that every person was thirsty for God's life," replied the store owner.

The young man took in the words with respectful skepticism. "*Every* person?" he said.

Mrs. Carter nodded.

This was probably no time to argue the point, Bertie thought to himself. Christians were all alike, thinking their religion was the only one and that everyone ought to believe it. He wasn't interested in the religious angle to this piece. He wanted to uncover *why* Dolan had shot her.

"It sounds like she was quite a young lady," he said noncommittally.

"If you really want to understand Lynne Jefferson, Mr. Snow, and want to know about that little Testament she was holding, I suggest you attend her memorial service tomorrow."

"Hmm...yeah, maybe I will.—Where is it?"

"At Destiny Junction Community Church...on Cedar Street."

"All right. Well...thanks for your time," said Snow.

The reporter left the store, thinking that he hadn't got much for his story. But he could tell that lady was bad news. If he wasn't careful, she would probably start—what was it called?—*witnessing* to him.

And that he could do without.

Sean Schaeffer had hardly slept in seventy-two hours.

All he could mumble, all he could think, all he could cry out—he could hardly call it "prayer"—was, "Why, Lord...*why*! Why Lynne...why the best and most loving girl in all the world!"

It wasn't right...it wasn't fair!

How could he possibly face seminary after this? He'd come north to Destiny Junction during last week's break to propose, only for it to end with such a mindless and cruel tragedy.

What did seminary matter now? He couldn't possibly face the pastorate alone...without Lynne.

What did anything matter? What did *life* itself matter?

How could he ever believe in God's goodness again? How could God possibly be good? And if he lost his belief in that, it was just a short step further before he lost his belief altogether.

Sean buried his face in his hands, his eyes flooding with tears of anguish.

"God, help me," he whispered. "I don't want to lose my faith...but part of me just doesn't care anymore."

Heather Fellowes tentatively walked toward the church. A thousand sensations and memories from childhood rushed back upon her.

She looked at the sign: *Destiny Junction Community Church*.

She had never been here before, yet it was all so familiar.

She walked inside and glanced around. She even recognized the churchy smell, the faint reminders of potlucks, nurseries, mildew and coffee. She knew, from the way she was dressed, that she looked out of place.

She walked forward in the direction of the office.

"I would like to see Pastor Jefferson," she said to the secretary behind the desk.

"I'm sorry, he's not in," the woman replied.

"I may have information...you know, about the shooting."

"Oh...oh, I see...I'll call him."

Heather waited.

Harlowe Jefferson walked through the door five minutes later. His secretary nodded to where Heather sat.

"Hello, I am Harlowe Jefferson," he said as he approached. "You are Miss—"

"Uh, just Heather," said Heather, standing up and shaking his offered hand.

"Please...come into my office."

He led and she followed him inside. He left the door open and offered her a chair.

"My secretary said you had information about my daughter's death," said the minister.

Heather nodded. "I was there," she said. "Well, not exactly *there*...but I heard what happened."

"You...do you mean you actually saw it?" he asked.

"No, but I live in a hotel on First Street...and my window was open. I heard everything...then I called the police."

"You?" said Jefferson in surprise. "They termed it an unidentified caller."

"That was me."

"I see," nodded the pastor. "Well...I would be very interested to know what happened."

Briefly Heather recounted the incident as it had burned itself into her memory. When she was through, both sat some moments in silence. Clearly moved by what he had heard, at length the minister nodded and smiled.

"I cannot tell you how much it means to me that you came here today," he said. "I can see that it was difficult for you."

Heather forced a thin smile of her own.

"Do you mind if I mention this tomorrow at the memorial service?" he asked.

"No...I suppose not," replied Heather.

"I hope you will be able to come. It will be here at the church at two o'clock."

"I'll see...maybe I will."

A little before four o'clock that same afternoon, Sally Parker wandered into the same shop Bertie Snow had left three hours before. The Answer Place, she thought as the door closed behind her. An odd name for a store.

"Good afternoon," a friendly voice greeted her before she had entirely gotten her bearings. "How are you today?"

"Uh…good, fine," Sally answered, glancing toward it. "I heard you carried cards."

"Yes, just there to your left, against the wall."

"Oh…I see them now—thank you."

She made her way toward the bank of fixtures and began perusing those featuring photographs. Lost in thought, a few minutes later she again heard the voice that had greeted her before.

"They're beautiful, aren't they?" said the lady as she approached. "I just discovered that line a short time ago. We've only had them a few weeks."

"Yes…I'm looking for card ideas. I like these."

"Ideas, how do you mean?"

"I design cards of my own—on computer, you know. Roses and nature photos mostly."

"Are these yours?" asked the woman, glancing at the proof sheet in her hand.

"Yes. I scan them in, then add a poem or something. I like to make the cards I send personal."

"These are beautiful. You're a very gifted photographer."

"Thank you," replied Sally, though a strange smile of sadness accompanied the words. "What kind of store is this anyway?" she said, glancing about. "It feels different than a regular card shop."

"It's a Christian bookstore."

"Oh…I hadn't realized. I've heard of Bible bookstores but I've never been inside one. I thought all they had were Bibles."

The lady smiled, though her expression too was tinged with sadness. The thought of Bibles reminded her of one of her favorite customers who would not be buying Bibles from her again.

"We do carry Bibles," she said, "and church supplies. But these days a Christian bookstore is much more than that."

"It's...it's really nice. I like the music," said Sally. "Do you mind if I look around after I'm through with the cards?"

"Of course not. There's a chair over there too if you want to sit down. Stay as long as you like."

With eyes that had been red on and off for days, Harlowe Jefferson rose from his knees and slumped into his chair. The new information he had recently learned from his strange young visitor sent him into a renewal of grief and prayerful reflection on the memorial service that was now less than twenty-four hours away.

Tomorrow he would stand in front of the church to remember and honor his only child. What was he going to say?

His heart was aching. What would *Lynne* want him to say?

He knew the answer well enough. She would want him to speak not about *her*, but to the people who came, and tell them about what it meant to be a Christian.

That young lady who had left his office forty minutes ago.... He could not escape the feeling that she was from a Christian home. But to look at her now...she was so lost, so hungry, so alone.

If Lynne had the chance, what would she say...*to her*, to that lost lamb named Heather?

Perhaps Lynne *did* have such a chance. Perhaps through her life, Lynne could still speak. Something told him that his cryptic visitor would be there tomorrow. And who could tell how many others whose lives Lynne had touched.

What would Lynne say to each one?

People he didn't even know...but who had had *some* connection with his daughter. How many might God draw to the service, each for his or her own private reasons?

What would Lynne say to them all?

Slowly Harlowe Jefferson opened his Bible to the Gospels and began scanning its pages.

When men revile you and persecute you and say all manner of evil against you, rejoice and be glad, for great is your reward in heaven.

Lynne had been persecuted. She had faced the *ultimate* persecution. What legacy had she left behind for him to convey to those who came?

God, he prayed, *give me Your words. Bring good of this in the lives of all those whom Lynne touched in some way.*

Twelve

2:00 P.M.

The memorial service for Lynne Jefferson was scheduled for Wednesday afternoon at Destiny Junction Community Church.

Pastor and Mrs. Jefferson had contacted Channel 3 with the request that the time and place be announced, which Leslie Cahill had done during Monday evening's newscast. On Tuesday the Jeffersons ran a quarter page ad in the local *Standard*, with a picture of their daughter and an open invitation to the service.

When Wednesday came, the church was more crowded than some of the members had ever seen it, a third of those present not knowing what had prompted them to come. Many were not churchgoers and had never met Lynne Jefferson personally. Yet the week's events had given rise to new and undefined feelings within them. They found themselves both curious, and somehow compelled to pay their respects. People filed quietly into the church—all coming for different reasons, drawn by invisible and unfamiliar stirrings.

At 2:05, when it appeared everyone had arrived and was seated, Lynne's father rose and walked to the pulpit.

"*My wife Anne and I are glad you have all come,*" he began. "*We gather today not to mourn the loss of our daughter, but rather to remember her life, and that greater Life to which she was so energetically devoted. We will*

81

surely shed tears, and you may weep with us. At the same time, however, as difficult as it is, we celebrate what Lynne stood for, and what her years among us meant."

He paused a moment, drawing in a breath.

"I will not deceive you," he went on. *"it is very difficult. Anne and I are grief-stricken. I cannot say we have not cried out to God many times during these past days, 'Why…why us…why Lynne!' We are human, and we doubt and ache and weep and mourn. Yet by faith we believe in God's goodness in the midst of tragedy.*

"No, my friends, we may not always see goodness amidst our mourning. But we determine to focus our thoughts and prayers toward God's ultimate purpose. This is a day filled with grief for the flesh. Yet we believe it is a day when circumstances compel us to look instead toward eternity."

The minister paused to take another breath. He was obviously experiencing deep emotions. His eyes scanned the sea of faces before him. The church was crowded to overflowing. Many of those present he had never seen before. Two rows were forced to stand behind the last pew for lack of space.

Charles Sweet stood listening at the back of the church where he was one of many the pastor did not recognize.

The crusty twenty-six year veteran of the Destiny Junction police force shifted once or twice on his feet. He had come today feeling it his duty. After all, he had been the first person on the scene after the shooting. Even if there had been a seat available when he'd walked in, he probably wouldn't have taken it. He was most comfortable when standing aloof and detached, expressionless—like many men, a spectator of life.

Eternity was not his beat. Leave that to the sky pilots and women.

He was a cop. He did not like to get personally involved.

But now as he stood in suit and tie, he felt strangely vulnerable without the protective facade of his blue uniform.

He shifted his weight nervously, and tried to divert his attention to something else.

Why were they here, Harlowe Jefferson wondered. What had drawn them? How had Lynne's life crossed the paths of these individuals? What private stories did each have to tell?

After a moment, the pastor went on.

"We would like to talk to you about our daughter Lynne," he continued. *"Lynne believed in something, believed in it enough that she gave her life for it. That something was this:*

"Lynne believed that every man and every woman urgently need to live in intimate relationship with the God who created them...the God who is their Father."

He paused and smiled, then added, *"She sometimes used to laugh and say, 'They need God, but most people don't know it!'"*

Bertie Snow began to wonder if coming here had been such a good idea. He'd thought maybe he could pick up an angle for his story to contrast with the up-close interview with Dolan. He had been trained in the Catholic tradition. But this was starting to sound like a fundamentalist revival service. Unfortunately, there didn't seem to be any chance of making a quick getaway from where he sat in the middle of a pew, surrounded on both sides by people and knees.

While the journalist squirmed in his seat, Lynne's father went on. *"My daughter's mission in life,"* he said, *"was to stir people up so they would recognize this need. That's what she saw as her reason for being on this earth— to stir people to look inside themselves and ask, 'What is life all about?'*

"You may be such a one whom she stirred in some way. I do not doubt that there are those among you whom she gave a tract..."

Tracey Keane, market checkout clerk, glanced down at the folded paper in her hand. It was the leaflet Lynne Jefferson had given her just the day before her death. She had read it over four or five times since then.

As she sat Tracey opened it again. The words were already familiar, almost as if they were being spoken by Lynne Jefferson herself. She didn't know who had written this little paper, but the words could have been intended just for her.

"How I gave my heart to Jesus Christ," she read again, "and found purpose and meaning in the midst of a lonely life..."

She hardly heard Mr. Jefferson's next words.

"...or whom she invited to church, or whom she gave a Bible or Testament..."

Bruce Penley had come into the church at one minute till two, feeling very out of place. He now stood in back with other men who looked far more presentable.

He had no church clothes. But he'd taken a shower and shaved at the mission to get some of the grime and smell off him. He knew people were wondering what he was doing there.

In the pocket of his scruffy coat his right hand clutched the Testament Lynne Jefferson had given him. He'd read it every day since that night on the sidewalk.

The poor kid, he thought, sending the back of a rough hand unconsciously across his eyes. She didn't deserve this.

"Lynne believed that every human being," her father said, *"each in his or her own unique way, was thirsty for the life God desired to give.*

"That thirst is felt in different ways," he went on. *"Yet strange to say, some are not aware they are thirsty at all, even though they may be dying for lack of spiritual water.*

"How do you get people to recognize their need, Lynne often asked me, when they don't think they need anyone but themselves?"

When Annette Gonzales arrived back in Destiny Junction after Sam's colon surgery, she was afraid. What if the surgery and chemo weren't successful? She knew the odds. Though all the doctors tried to sound upbeat, between the lines on their faces she knew they were not optimistic about Sam's chances.

She would leave for Chambers again tomorrow. Hopefully they would release Sam and let him come home.

For the past few days all she could think of was Sam and his condition. But today as she sat listening, for some strange reason her *own* mortality began to stare her in the face. It was the first time she had been to church in a long while. All at once Annette found herself wondering about eternity. Then followed the question she realized she had been avoiding.

Was Sam actually going to die?

She had never thought about such things before. All at once she knew she could postpone it no longer. If Sam was going to die, she wanted him to be prepared.

And since she was on the subject, there was one more thing she needed to ask.

Was *she* ready to die?

Were either of them ready to meet God and account for their lives on this earth?

"Every single individual on the face of the earth," Pastor Jefferson went on, *"every one of us shares this thirst—rich and poor, young and old, men and women...everyone. It is what one of the great philosophers called the 'God-shaped vacuum in every soul.'*

"I am not much of a philosopher myself. I am a practical man. Lynne was practical and down-to-earth too. But I do know something about being hungry and thirsty. They are practical sensations we all feel. In a way, hunger and thirst are the most practical things in all the world. Maybe that's why Jesus used those terms to describe our need for God."

Barbara Kingston wept not only for Lynne Jefferson, daughter of her friend the pastor's wife, but also because her Tom should be hearing this.

But he was in the city on business…again. Why did he have to be gone *now*? She had almost talked him into coming to the service with her. Then at the last minute he had changed his mind and driven into Chambers.

It was so frustrating. It seemed whenever there was a message perfectly aimed at Tom, he wasn't in church. How would he ever get right with the Lord if he was never there to hear?

God, wherever Tom is, she silently prayed, *draw him to You*.

Gradually the minister's voice intruded again into Barbara's hearing.

"The reason this hole, this vacuum, this thirst exists in each of us," he was saying, *"is that God left behind a little piece of Himself in our hearts when He created us. It is like a tiny invisible spiritual homing device that is always pointing us back in the direction of our Maker. It is what makes us different from the lower animals.*

"It is what we call the soul."

As Doug Taggart listened, the pastor's words probed uncomfortably into regions he was not accustomed to exploring.

He had everything that was supposed to bring you happiness in life— money, prestige, influence. Why did he suddenly feel that maybe his life *wasn't* counting for the most important things after all?

What if suddenly he found himself on his deathbed, what would his bank and stock portfolio matter then? He was fifty-six years old and had put on more weight than he wanted to admit. And though he had not told his wife, his blood pressure had been up a little at his last physical. They were the kinds of things men in his position always tried to convince themselves wouldn't come calling for yet a while longer. He'd attend to his weight, his blood pressure, and his soul…later.

But what if *later* had finally arrived?

"That in a nutshell is what Lynne's life was about," said the pastor. *"That is why John 7:37 was one of her favorite verses in the Bible.*

"Eleven short words: 'If anyone is thirsty, let him come to Me and drink.'

"It is a simple principle, yet a profound truth upon which Lynne based everything she did. Her purpose in life was nothing more nor less than to tell people where to find the water of life."

Margaret Sanderson sat with tears in her eyes. Her encounter with Lynne Jefferson had been so brief. Yet as she recalled it, that's just what the short incident had been for her—like a refreshing cool mountain stream...clear, bright, sparkling.

Lynne had given her water to drink, even if only just a passing sip.

Perhaps it was time for her to find the source of that water for herself.

"I remember Lynne saying to me often, however, 'Daddy, it is so sad that people don't know they need God. They're too proud and satisfied with their lives to admit they need anyone, especially God. I don't understand pride, Daddy. What's the big deal with admitting you need God in your life?'"

Another pause came, while Dr. Jefferson collected his thoughts.

At the word *pride*, where she sat listening Carole Laudine felt an invisible knife plunge straight into her heart like a red-hot iron. Why did she react so? It was as if the man knew all about her and had in that instant undressed her soul.

She had gone to Stanford on a full scholarship as one of its most promising new students, one of those rare individuals who could have excelled in any of a number of fields.

By the time she received her Ph.D. at the age of 26, she had more offers on the table from prestigious universities than she knew what to do with. But from the very first day when she knew she wanted to teach, she had determined to give at least two or three years to Northwestern, the small college where her father had taught for so many years. Now she was making good on that commitment in the small town where she had grown up. The offers would still be there whenever she wanted them, and teaching at Northwestern had also given her the freedom to work on her first book, which was now in its final stages of completion.

She had had things her own way for so long, feminist Carole Laudine was used to being the center of attention wherever she went. She heard people *ooh* and *ah* when she spoke. They glanced up when she entered a room. Simply put, she had come to think more than a little highly of herself.

But last week Lynne Jefferson had pricked something deep, calling her up short, challenging her prejudices. Why did God-talk bother her so? Was she just as biased against Christians as she had always accused them of being toward others? It was a disturbing possibility.

Her...Carole Laudine...prejudiced and proud?

And now Lynne's father seemed intent on continuing the filleting of her soul as he repeated Lynne's piercing words...*it is so sad that people don't know they need God...too proud to admit they need anyone...what's the big deal with admitting you need God in your life.*

"Lynne believed something else that is equally important," Mr. Jefferson continued. *"She believed that the Bible was true and practical for today.*

"We have a store in our town whose owner was a dear friend of Lynne's and is with us today. It is called The Answer Place.

"Lynne Jefferson believed that the Bible was the answer place—that its pages contained both truth and answers—truth that explains the universe and daily practical answers for the sufferings, hardships and confusions of everyday life.

"Truth and answers. That's why Lynne called the Bible her guidebook for living."

Where she sat listening, Sally Parker still wasn't sure why she'd come. She hadn't gone to church once since moving to Destiny Junction three years ago. She'd never heard of Lynne Jefferson before the shooting. But yesterday she had seen the notice of the service at the Christian bookstore.

And after picking up the newspaper and reading a brief article about the shooting, then seeing another invitation to the service, something told her she ought to attend.

She had remained in the Christian bookstore over an hour yesterday. She'd felt such strange warm vibrations while there. The atmosphere was so inviting and peaceful.

It didn't feel like a store at all. And the nice good-bye from the owner when she'd left, like they were old friends, "I hope you'll come back!" was so sincere. The lady seemed to really mean it.

Sally was not used to being cared about. Why would a stranger show interest in a single customer she'd never laid eyes on before?

As the pastor's words intruded again into her ears, she could not help wondering what he would say to *her*. Or was all this just for "normal" people—people who didn't have to deal with the kinds of hidden secrets that plagued her?

Did the Bible have *answers* for one whose father had sexually molested her from the time she was five until high school?

She could hardly imagine it. Answers...maybe—for *most* problems. But not for this kind of stuff.

They said God was love.

But could God really love someone like *her*?

"That's how Lynne saw the Bible," her father continued. *"She read God's Word to understand life, the world, people and herself. And she read it to discover how to live. She read it for the big things and the little things— and for everything in between."*

Pastor Jefferson paused for several long seconds.

Dixie Judd was trying to remember that little paper Lynne Jefferson had given her a year ago. She thought it might have had something to do with what the pastor was talking about.

That's probably why she had thrown it away. Who cared about the meaning of the universe? She had enough trouble just paying her bills.

But she could use some answers, that was for sure. Life had been rough since her divorce.

"Now to those of you not accustomed to listening to me every week," Lynne's father went on, *"these last few minutes may have seemed too much like a sermon to suit you. But I have a good reason for telling you those things. We have come here to remember Lynne Jefferson. But what will that mean if we do not pay attention to what she lived for? To honor her means to honor what she believed. So I am going to ask every one of you here today, in the quietness of your own hearts, to consider whether you have been attentive enough to the thirst in your own soul.*

"Because if Lynne could say one thing to you right now, that is what she would say."

Brock Yates wondered what he was doing here. He'd seen the announcement posted at school yesterday when he and Yvonne were walking at lunch. He remembered the strange effect Lynne's face had on him when watching the news on TV last Saturday.

"Did you see that girl here last week?" Yvonne had said, almost as if she were reading his thoughts.

"No...no, why—was she at school?"

"Yeah, she invited me and Jill to that Bible Club thing."

Ordinarily some wisecrack might have come out of Brock's mouth at the mention of the Bible Club. But not today.

"What do you think," he said as they continued on, "you want to go to that service they're having for her tomorrow?"

"You mean for the girl that got killed?"

"Yeah."

"Hmm…Jill goes to some youth group at that church. She said she was going."

"Maybe we should go with her?"

"I don't know…sure, maybe that'd be cool."

And now, with permission to leave school early in order to attend, here they were.

The football star's attention returned to the sound of the pastor's voice.

"What I would like you to do to honor the memory of Lynne Jefferson," said the pastor, *"is to go home and open a Bible to four verses in the Gospel of John—the one I already mentioned, John 7:37, and also from John 3 the third verse and the sixteenth verse, and John 10:10. If you do not have a Bible, come see me and I will get you one. I want to ask you to read these passages honestly and prayerfully and then say to God, 'Show me Your truth. Reveal Yourself to me. Show me my thirst and my need for You. And teach me how to live the abundant life that Lynne Jefferson lived.'*

"And I am going to ask those of you who are Christians or churchgoers, to consider whether you have been sufficiently attentive to the Bible too, whether you are in the habit of going to God's Word both for big truth and for everyday answers."

Newscaster Leslie Cahill thought to herself, When was the last time I read the Bible?

Who was she trying to kid? She had *never* actually sat down and read it. She had heard it quoted and read bits and pieces for Lit class. But she couldn't remember ever just reading it.

Come to think of it…did she even *have* a Bible?

"I am asking you all, and I include myself," Mr. Jefferson went on, *"to do what Lynne would want us to do if she were here—discover the life-changing truth and power of God's Word, each of us in our own ways.*

"A relationship with God and His Son Jesus is not something that is just for so-called religious types. It is for everyone. Children, lawyers, garbage collectors, doctors, teachers, students, politicians, businesspersons, as well as the homeless and unemployed. Yes, and even modern, free-thinking, self-sufficient, independent-minded men and women who may seem to have it all together without needing anyone. You, my friend—whoever you are—need this relationship. You might not know it, you might not have ever considered such a thing before...but you need friendship with Jesus Christ. Not as a crutch, not as a mere 'extra' in life, but as an essential, fundamental requirement of life."

Jill Chin sat next to Yvonne and her boyfriend, sick with guilt. The last time she had seen Lynne alive was at school last Friday. But when she and Yvonne ran into her, she had been too embarrassed to go to Bible Club with Lynne, or even acknowledge that they knew each other. Yvonne had laughed at the idea, and Jill had joined in nervously, too timid to stand up for her faith, too timid even to tell Yvonne later that Lynne Jefferson was a friend from church. She had glanced back a moment later, hoping to catch Lynne's eyes as if to somehow make up for her callousness. But she was already talking to that Tolek girl.

Jill had never seen her alive again. She was a Christian coward, nothing more. Her stomach was tied up in knots over it.

She could never make up for what had happened. But maybe it was time she took a good hard look at how serious she really was about being a Christian.

"You would not have come here unless you felt you wanted somehow to honor the memory of our daughter. I am asking you to do so by reading these verses and asking what meaning they have in your life."

Dr. Sarah Woo had known the Jeffersons for a long time. She liked them, respected them. But she had always considered them somehow different than ordinary people.

Harlowe Jefferson was a minister, after all. Anne was a minister's wife. That set them apart. Ministers were *supposed* to be religious.

But she was a doctor. She dealt with practical realities, with life and...

Suddenly Sarah Woo's train of thought stopped abruptly in its tracks.

The word *death* came slowly into her mind.

Was the reality of *death* perhaps the point where the practicality of *life* intersected with the larger meaning of religion?

If that were true, perhaps the distinction between her own profession and the minister's was not as great as she had assumed.

Dr. Woo recalled staring down at Lynne's body, touching her face, still warm, knowing that just minutes before she had passed across that mysterious threshold no physician on earth could understand...from life into what is called eternity.

What did that *mean*? What had she experienced?

And where was Lynne Jefferson...now?

Perhaps as a physician she ought to have paid more attention to such things. Maybe it was time she began.

Mr. Jefferson now held up the New Testament that was in his hand.

"As you know, Lynne was clutching this little book, her finger at the page of John 3:16, when she died. I want to ask you all now to pray for Hank Dolan, the man who has been arrested in the shooting."

In the back of the church, one man was even more noticeably out of place than Bruce Penley and Charlie Sweet, judging from the look in his eyes. Wolf Griswold stood stoically beside the policeman, neither cop nor hit man aware of the other's profession. He had come today hoping to gain some information about Dolan.

But to pray for him!

An evil smile cracked Griswold's lips. Yeah, he would pray for him all right, then put a bullet in his head!

"Even as I heard about the incident," said Lynne's father, now fighting tears, *"I thought to myself that it would not surprise me to learn that she was praying for the man even as he took her life. I knew that to be the kind of thing Lynne would do. And as it turns out, I was not so far wrong. For just twenty-four hours ago I learned..."*

Where Heather Fellowes listened, she remembered her few minutes in the minister's office yesterday. She had been the only one besides Dolan who knew what happened...the only one who had heard the last words ever to come from Lynne Jefferson's mouth. She knew she had to attend the service for no other reason than that. And now as the girl's father recounted their conversation, she relived the terrible sounds of that day all over again in her memory.

"Shut up," she heard Dolan's angry voice on the street below.

"I am going to pray for you, Mr. Dolan," returned Lynne in a calm and steady voice, "because God loves you."

"Shut up, I tell you!" yelled Dolan. "If you say another word, God help you—I'll kill you!"

"Dear Jesus," came the soft voice again, "I pray right now for Hank's soul, that he will come to know You as his—"

The next sound to explode in Heather Fellowes' ear was the sharp blast from Dolan's pistol. She jumped from her bed and ran to the window, just in time to see his retreating form running into an alley. Below her window lay the body of the young woman whose words of prayer had cost her her life.

"That is what happened," came Rev. Jefferson's voice again into Heather's thoughts. *"The individual who heard it is with us today.*

"And the question I have been asking myself once I heard what happened is this: Can we do less than Lynne was willing to do?

"We must pray for him. Our Lord commands it of us, and if the day should come, by a miracle of God's grace, that this man gives his heart to the Lord because of those prayers, Lynne would be the first to rejoice and say that her life was not lived in vain.

"Finally," said Jefferson, *"let me close by reading a brief poem Lynne wrote. It is enscribed inside this Testament. Perhaps one of you is here today with a Bible or Testament with these words from Lynne's hand inside it."*

Lidia Tolek sat listening, remembering last Friday when Lynne Jefferson had given her a little Testament at school just like her father said. As he now read the words, Lidia took the small book out of her purse, opened it, and read along with the words Lynne had written to her.

She wished Trent was here. He was so messed up, he needed to hear this.

Harlowe Jefferson proceeded to read the inscription that Lynne had written in the Testament intended for Hank Dolan at the counter of the store just a few days earlier.

"The Bible is truth, for it is God's book.
To quench life's thirst, in its pages we must look.
Open it, read it, and you will find
an abundant life meant for all mankind.
But the greatest news of all, and to you I say,
is that it's true for you, if you'll only obey.
How can I know this truth you speak of?
Where do I meet this God you call love?
He's not far to seek if you'll but make a start.
In fact, you'll discover Him in your very own heart.
That's where He will dwell if you'll open the door,
and by invitation make Him your personal Savior.
So take God at His word, put His truth to the test,
open your heart to Him, let His Spirit do the rest.
Again I remind you—please, hear me through:
The Bible is true, and God's love is for you!"

Thirteen

Thursday, October 23

6:16 a.m.

When Sally Parker awoke the following morning, the sound that had ended her dream with visions of a robed man knocking on a door, now came from outside her window.

She rolled over, then sat up and pulled back the window curtain. The woodpecker was up in the oak again.

She watched as he whacked away at the bark. Then, just like yesterday, one of the few remaining leaves on the branch just above the bird's head suddenly released and gently fell. It landed a moment later amid a thousand others just like it now rotting on the ground.

What a great photo opportunity!

Sally threw off the covers, pulled on sweats over her nightshirt, crammed her bare toes into sneakers lying beside the bed, grabbed her camera from the desk, and hurried downstairs and outside.

Ten minutes later, with half a roll of pictures taken, she turned with a shivering smile and ran back to the warmth inside.

She entered the kitchen to put water on for tea. Suddenly the simple realization dawned on her that she had been feeling *happy*.

What was the last time she had felt such pleasure as the sight of the woodpecker and falling leaves had just generated? What could explain it?

She placed the teakettle on the stove. Could what she felt have anything to do with yesterday's service for the Jefferson girl? She recalled what the girl's father had said about asking people to look up those four Bible verses. She couldn't remember what they were, and she didn't even own a Bible anyway.

Maybe she ought to go back to that store and ask about them. She had seen the store owner across the church at the service. She would probably know what the verses were.

———◦◦◦———

From where Margaret Sanderson watched the photographer, her thoughts, too, were on yesterday's service. How remarkable it was that her life could have been so affected in such a short time by a chance encounter with someone she didn't even know.

She smiled as she saw the young woman across the way hurry inside. She would like to see some of those pictures.

———◦◦◦———

Jill Chin arrived at school thinking about sitting in church yesterday with Yvonne and Brock.

She would never have imagined such a thing possible, yet they had asked to go with her. The homecoming king and queen…in church with *her*!

Ever since, a new thought had kept her awake almost the whole night: Should she invite them to church on Sunday? *Real* church…with music, Bible reading, prayer and a sermon?

The thought of Yvonne laughing in her face at the suggestion wasn't pleasant. Yet Jill had the feeling she was supposed to do it.

She rounded a corner of the hall. A girl was walking toward her. Jill slowed and gave a half smile.

"Uh, hi…didn't I see you at the memorial service yesterday?"

The girl stopped. "Yes," she said, "I was there."

"Did you know Lynne Jefferson?"

"No, not really...I mean, I'd just met her once, when she was here at the school a week ago."

"Oh, that's right—now I remember seeing you with her."

Jill paused. "I'm sorry," she said, "I know I should remember, but I've forgotten your name."

"Lidia."

"Oh, yes...that's right. Hi, Lidia—I'm Jill."

Barbara Kingston stood in her bedroom holding a piece of paper that had fallen from the pocket of Tom's trousers when she had been going through his things to do a load of laundry. Tears streamed down her face.

How could she have been such a fool as to think his quietness lately was due to a spiritual awakening?

She couldn't believe it—this could not be happening! It was too awful...her own husband...and another woman!

Her stomach felt like she was going to be sick. And all those late-night meetings! Was he with her right now?

"Oh, God," she cried at the thought. "What am I going to do?!"

As she drove to the station, Leslie Cahill tried to put the spiritual implications of the memorial service out of her mind.

This was a news scoop. She had no time to be thinking about her soul right now. She had to find out the identity of that witness and get an interview. She would go see Pastor Jefferson today.

Two hours later she was sitting in the pastor's office with Lynne Jefferson's father. She had just explained her request.

"I understand your point, Miss Cahill," the minister said. "But I'm sure you see that I cannot divulge the identity of the individual who came to me without his or her consent. What I will do, however, is attempt to convey what you have asked and ask if they would consider speaking with you."

"I appreciate that, Mr. Jefferson," said Cahill, rising. "Could I give you my telephone number? In case the person agrees, tell them to feel free to call."

"I see no harm in that."

Cahill took out one of her cards and handed it to him. "And let me tell you again how very sorry I am about your daughter," she said.

"Thank you."

The newscaster turned to leave, then hesitated.

"You know, there is one other thing I would like to ask," she said. "At the service yesterday, you mentioned several verses in the Bible. I would like to read them, to help me understand this story more completely. But when I got home I realized, I am embarrassed to say, that I didn't even have a Bible. I was wondering—"

"Say no more," smiled the pastor. "I would be happy to let you borrow one."

He turned and picked up a book from the shelf behind him.

"Would you mind writing down the verses for me?" she asked.

"Not at all," replied Jefferson. "You'll be able to find the books easily enough in the table of contents. If you have any questions about what you've read, please do not hesitate to come see me again."

Annette Gonzales sat on the edge of her bed in the bedroom with their three young girls. She had been trying to explain the reason for their sudden frequent trips into the city, and why their father had to be in the hospital.

"Is Daddy going to die?" asked the older of the girls, herself only eight.

Annette blinked hard to fight back the sudden stinging in her eyes at the abruptness of the question. Even though it was the very thing at the forefront of her own mind for days, her daughter's blunt honesty brought fresh tears. She tried to smile reassuringly.

"No, dear. The doctors are working very hard to help him," she said. "And we must all pray very hard that God will heal Daddy's cancer."

"I don't want Daddy to die," said the youngest, now starting to cry.

Annette reached over and took her in her arms, then stretched another hand out to draw in the other two in a comforting motherly embrace.

———◦◦◦———

In Chambers, Tom Kingston had no idea that back in Destiny Junction his wife had discovered the note in a strange but obviously feminine hand.

Tom followed Michelle into the motel room noticeably ill at ease.

"You've hardly said two words all day," she said, taking off her coat.

Tom shrugged.

Michelle sat down on the bed and took off her shoes.

"What is it?" she said.

"I don't know," replied Tom.

Slowly he glanced around as she continued to undress.

"I'm sorry," he said after a moment, "I just can't do this today."

She paused and looked up. "What's wrong?" she asked. "You're not yourself."

"I don't know. I just think I need to get home. Sorry...I'll call you."

He turned and left the room, leaving the young secretary staring after him, not knowing whether to be concerned or irritated.

———◦◦◦———

Carole Laudine sat in her office at Northwestern trying to collect her thoughts and organize her notes for her next class.

But she was too distracted to think.

The words from yesterday had remained in her heart like red-hot accusing lumps of coal...*pride, pride, pride.* Was she too proud to admit that *she* might actually need God?

It was a thought she could hardly face. But once let loose, a thought she could not keep from haunting her. Self-sufficient, self-assured, attractive

Carole Laudine, the most sought-after single woman on the faculty of the college…she had always figured religion was only for life's losers and weaklings. What in the world was *she* doing thinking about God?

———◦◦◦———

That same afternoon Sally Parker again found herself approaching The Answer Place. She went inside and walked to the counter.

"Hello again," said Jeanne Carter, greeting her.

"I saw you at the memorial service yesterday," Sally began. "I wondered if you could answer a question. Do you remember when the minister talked about those four verses?"

Jeanne nodded.

"Do you remember what they were?" asked Sally. "I would like to read them, but I don't have a Bible."

"Of course," replied Jeanne. "All were from the Gospel of John. John 3:3, 3:16, 7:37 and 10:10." She jotted them down on a piece of paper.

"Is there a Bible I could look them up in?"

"Certainly, use any one in the store you like."

"Why don't you pick one for me."

The store owner walked toward the Bible alcove, picked one of the newer translations from the shelves and handed it to Sally.

"The Gospel of John…that's toward the back, right?" she said as she took it.

"Yes, it's the fourth book of the New Testament. Here—I'll show you."

Jeanne took the Bible again, quickly opened it to the beginning of John's Gospel, then handed it back to Sally.

"Why don't you have a seat over there," she pointed. "Just make yourself comfortable and take as long as you like."

Sally sat down, then began scanning the pages in front of her to locate the third chapter. When Jeanne glanced over a few minutes later, she saw Sally engrossed in the book.

When the owner next looked up, Sally was again approaching the counter. She handed Jeanne the Bible.

"Thank you," she said. "I probably should buy a Bible. Is that a good one?"

Jeanne nodded. "But there are many to choose from…in different translations, different bindings and sizes. If you are serious about wanting a new Bible, what I would recommend is that you take thirty minutes or so reading in several and comparing them. That way you can get a feel for which translation you like."

"I would like to do that," said Sally. "But I have to get back to work now—I'm on my lunch hour. I'll come back and do what you say."

She paused, then smiled a little awkwardly.

"Do you mind if I ask you one more question?" she said.

"Of course not," replied Jeanne.

"In one of those verses I read, it talked about a more *abundant* life. What does that mean?"

"Life as a Christian…life with Jesus. One of the other translations calls it 'life to the full.' I like that. That's what life with Jesus is—it's life to the full."

"Is that what being born again means, like the other verse said?"

"That's how one enters into life with Jesus, being born again."

"How do you do that?"

"By asking His Spirit to come into your heart and live there."

"That's all?"

"There's nothing complicated about becoming a Christian."

"Hmm…I see," nodded Sally. "Well, you've given me a lot to think about. I've got to get going. But I'll be in again."

"The Lord bless you," said Jeanne after her.

As Sally Parker left, thoughts of the few church experiences she had had in her childhood came back to her, misconceptions that seemed so different than the warm and simple brand of Christianity she felt whenever she went into The Answer Place. The lady there did not remind her of the hellfire and brimstone religion she had always associated with Christianity.

She was different. Something other than fear of hell was surely the reason she was a Christian.

Fourteen

Sunday, October 26

8:37 A.M.

Bertie Snow woke early and read over his story again from several days ago as he sipped at his morning coffee.

Stale, he thought. He'd been too eager to rush it into print on the heels of Lynne Jefferson's shooting. He'd gotten the facts right. But the story behind the story, he'd missed it. He now realized it clearly enough.

He was still an amateur, Bertie reflected morosely. He wanted so badly to make it to the big time. But if this was any indication of his skill, he wasn't ready.

He'd have to try again. Write another piece. Dig deeper. Uncover something he had missed before. If he was ever going to be any good as a journalist, he had to find the *real* story.

He would have to go back to that church again.

Tracey Keane slept in till eight.

She had this Sunday off. But one day was just the same as another in her life. What did she need with a whole Sunday cooped up in her apartment? She wasn't interested in football. What was she going to do, watch some dumb movie on TV? Maybe she'd go to the mall.

Still in her robe, she absently picked up yesterday's paper, flopped down on the couch and began scanning it again. A few minutes later she tossed it aside. A piece of paper on the coffee table drew her eye. It was the leaflet from Lynne Jefferson. The thing seemed determined to keep haunting her every time she turned around. She'd read it so many times she practically knew it by heart.

She picked it up and perused it again. At the bottom—she'd hardly noticed it before—three lines had been rubber-stamped: *Hungry for life? Thirsty for meaning? Join us at Destiny Junction Community Church.*

Carole Laudine had set aside today to work on her book.

But the moment she sat down at her desk in her office at home, she knew it was no use. Her mind was distracted.

She didn't like to admit it, but she knew the reason why. It was all this business with Lynne Jefferson and the disconcerting memorial service.

Weekends were always hardest for Richard Ray. The streets seemed empty and lifeless. There was nothing to do. He'd go see Dixie in the café.

Lane Rakestraw had felt bad ever since that history class when it had dawned on him that there was something missing in what he had considered his Christianity. Then Leslie had asked him to go to the memorial service last Wednesday because she hadn't wanted to sit alone. He'd read his Bible a couple of times since, and when he woke up this morning, the strangest urge came over him to go to church.

Maybe it was about time he started being more regular again.

Lidia Tolek knew she wanted to go back to that church.

She woke up Sunday morning, took a shower and began looking through the closet for the nicest outfit she had.

"What are you all dressed up for?" asked her mom when she came in for breakfast.

"I thought I would go to church, is that okay?"

"Sure...which one?"

"I thought I'd walk over to the Community Church...you know, on Cedar."

"What do you want to go to church for?" grunted Trent as he walked in.

"I don't know," replied Lidia. "I just want to, that's all. You want to go with me?"

"Heck no," he answered.

———◦◦◦———

Jack Snow, deputy chief of police, woke up on Sunday morning with the strangest feeling. Today was the big game between the 49ers and the Cowboys. He had been looking forward to it for weeks. Yet inexplicably he felt like he ought to go to church.

He opened yesterday's paper to the church page ads.

Destiny Junction Community Church, he read in one of the small boxes, Harlowe Jefferson, Pastor.

That was the father of the girl who'd been killed. He'd give it a try... and pay his respects at the same time.

———◦◦◦———

Tom Kingston felt similar stirrings. He'd come home from Chambers with a bad feeling in the pit of his stomach. He had been trying to make up for his guilty conscience ever since. Barbara had said nothing, but an undefined anxiety told him she suspected something.

When Sunday morning came, after breakfast Tom began to put on his slacks and a dress shirt.

"Where are you going?" asked Barbara.

"I thought we'd go to church together, like you said."

"I thought there was an important game you were going to watch today."

"It's not that big a deal," replied Tom. "I'll catch the highlights tonight."

———◦◦◦———

Bruce Penley swallowed the last bite of scrambled eggs from his plate and washed the remains of his breakfast down with a long swallow of the rescue mission's bad coffee, then rose and headed for the door.

"Going to church today, Bruce?" called out the voice of one of the volunteers behind him.

"I don't know," he mumbled back over his shoulder. "I ain't much of a churchgoer."

"Might do you some good."

"Yeah, I suppose…I'll see."

Fifteen

SUNDAY, OCTOBER 26

10:48 A.M.

When the parking lot began to fill and people began to file through the door of Destiny Junction Community Church a little before eleven, it was obvious to the regular membership that something very unusual was going on. Every third or fourth person to walk in, it seemed, was a visitor.

What had drawn them here on this day was not so much on the minds of some of the men as where they were all going to sit. By ten till the hour, the four ushers and several deacons were scrambling back and forth from several of the Sunday school rooms with folding chairs to put in the back and along the rear in the balcony.

Many of the newcomers appeared nervous, not quite knowing what to expect. Attending a memorial service during the week was one thing. Coming to an actual Sunday morning worship service—that was something else altogether.

Waitress Dixie Judd followed history professor Carole Laudine inside, though the two did not know one another, and sat down beside her in a pew halfway toward the front. They made themselves comfortable, the one dressed in a skirt a little too short for the solemnity of the occasion, the other tastefully attired in an expensive professional-looking pantsuit. Several rows in front of them sat Tracey Keane alongside Sam and Annette Gonzales and their somber family. Behind them on the aisle, newscaster Leslie Cahill fidgeted nervously, the pastor's borrowed Bible in her lap, as she waited for the service to begin. Across the center aisle and still unknown to her sat Heather Fellowes, the very girl whom she had gone to Pastor Jefferson asking about. Three rows in front of Heather, Jill Chin sat with her friend Yvonne Seymour and Brock Yates, both of whom, to Jill's surprise, had accepted her invitation. Not far from Sean Schaeffer and Jim Franklin was Margaret Sanderson. She had walked her dog along the street behind the church hundreds of times hardly thinking a thing of it. Now here she was inside waiting for the service to begin. Toward the back sat insurance mogul Scott Peyton, who had come, not so much to pay his respects as to observe good business protocol.

Meanwhile, in the back more and more newcomers were walking slowly in along with Junction Community's regular membership. Bruce Penley shuffled haltingly through the doors, unaware that even his best set of clothes gave off an odor too strong to be drowned out by the many varieties of perfume and miscellaneous body emollients and hair products in evidence throughout the sanctuary. He was glad to see chairs at the back where he could hopefully blend in anonymously. Somewhat awkwardly, he headed toward them.

Richard Ray, to whom Dixie had mentioned her plans to come, walked in and looked about. But he was unable to distinguish that of his waitress friend from the hundred heads he saw already seated. Not wanting to brave such an intimidating spectacle as walking down the aisle looking for her, he headed instead for the balcony. As he took a seat a minute later, he had no idea that he was sitting next to Tom and Barbara Kingston, and that behind him, scattered about the several pews, also sat Sally Parker, Lidia Tolek, and Dr. Sarah Woo.

The large muscular form of Deputy Police Chief Jack Snow walked into the church feeling out of place. He hadn't darkened the door of a church for fifteen years.

"Hey, Charlie," he said softly, glad to see a familiar face and shaking the patrolman's hand, "I didn't know you were a churchman."

"I'm not, but...you know—the shooting," replied Sweet nervously over the organ music coming from the sanctuary. "I thought I ought to come."

"Yeah, me too."

Just then Snow saw his nephew moving past them toward one of the aisles.

"Bertie," he said after him.

The young journalist turned.

"Uncle Jack!" he exclaimed in a loud whisper, "what are you doing here?"

Snow leaned toward him and half shielded his mouth with the back of his hand. "I was about to ask you the same thing," he whispered.

"Covering a story...what's your excuse?"

"I don't suppose I have one—just felt like coming. Where you gonna sit? Mind if we join you?"

"Sure...that'd be fine."

"Do you know Charlie Sweet?"

"No, don't believe so."

"Bertie Snow...Charlie Sweet."

The policeman and the reporter shook hands, then headed toward the nearest aisle. All moved into the back row together and sat down. Patrolman Sweet scooted into the center next to banker Doug Taggart. The two had never met, but nodded to one another as Sweet settled in, then sat quietly waiting for the service to begin. Just behind them, on the first makeshift row of folding chairs, sat Lane Rakestraw.

All around them were other such men and women in ones and twos whom Lynne Jefferson's life had touched and who had found themselves inexplicably compelled to come here on this day.

—————◆◇◆—————

Ten minutes later Harlowe Jefferson walked slowly forward as the congregation noisily sat down following the singing of the opening hymn.

The pages of his prepared sermon were already in place on the lectern. He had dug the notes out of his file on Friday. With the events of the week just past, and the emotional stress of Wednesday's memorial service followed by the private graveside ceremony at the cemetery, there was no way he would have been able to come up with a new sermon for today. He hadn't preached this particular one in years, but it ought to do fine.

The moment he stood up in front of the church, however, he was shocked at what he saw. The sanctuary was packed with visitors. It was just like Wednesday—half the faces were ones he didn't recognize!

He had stumbled through the hymn, and now did his best with the opening prayer and announcements, his brain full of unconscious prayer. Was this somehow related to Lynne's death? *Why* had these people returned for today's service?

As the hour progressed, steadily the conviction grew upon him that there were *men and women* out there in the pews looking up at him who might not have been in church for years, many of whom might not know what it meant to be a Christian. Perhaps the Spirit had drawn them here, at this particular moment in time, to hear something different than a stale sermon on the text of the widow and the two mites.

As he took the pulpit to speak at about twenty-five minutes after the hour, Harlowe Jefferson stood for a moment gazing down at his typed sermon notes and realized that what he had planned was no longer appropriate. He turned the sheets over, then tried to collect his thoughts.

"Lord, I don't know what You have planned for today," he prayed silently. "I ask You to give me Your words for these who have come. Speak into their hearts, Lord, in spite of the weakness I feel at this moment."

He gazed over the congregation for several moments.

"*I would like to talk to you this morning,*" Jefferson began at length, "*about a topic that will be familiar to all of you, but which many people do not understand. I want to talk about one of the most oft-used words in our spiritual lexicon, yet a word that remains a mystery to many. I see that a number of you here today are new to us. Many of you may not be fully aware what this word actually means, though it is a word I am sure you are all familiar with.*"

Again he paused briefly. It was still not too late to return to the pre-pared text about the widow. But his inner debate lasted only a few seconds. He would plunge ahead.

"*That word is salvation,*" Harlowe Jefferson went on. "*I would like to discuss what it is, and how one enters into this experience that Christians call salvation.*"

As Pastor Jefferson continued, his words struck unexpectedly deep into the hearts of his listeners just as they had the previous Wednesday. His voice carried a strange power. Though none would have imagined that a sermon on salvation could hold them spellbound, not a muscle moved, not an eye wandered for the next sixteen minutes. His words hit home with uncanny precision. Nearly everyone listening could not help but reflect personally and inwardly on their own spiritual condition.

When he began what were obviously his concluding remarks, many unconsciously glanced down at their watches to see that they read quarter till twelve.

"*Many of you are no doubt aware,*" said the pastor, "*of the custom in many churches of making what is sometimes called an altar call, encourag-ing people to walk forward during the singing of a closing hymn. Some of you may have seen it during large televised crusades. But I am not going to do that today. I am only going to ask you to do one thing. No one else in all the world will know the result.*

"*That request is that you say to the Lord in your heart, either now or at a time when you can be alone, 'God, if I am such a person as he has been talking about, who needs to respond to You in one of these ways, please reveal it to me. Then show me what to do.'*

"*My friends, do not be afraid of the word prayer. All it means is talk-ing to God like you would anyone else. Aloud, silently, eyes open, eyes closed, in the daytime, at night, walking along a busy sidewalk or on your knees in your office or bedroom or kitchen...none of that matters.*

"*Talk to God. That is prayer.*

"No thees and thous and flowery old-fashioned language. Don't make an effort to pray in King James English. Just conversation, dialogue, honest communication with your heavenly Father. He is no giant, unsmiling ogre. He is your Father, and it is time you became acquainted with Him.

"If you will pray that prayer—either now or when you are alone later today or this evening or tomorrow or the next day—you can be sure that He will answer it.

"Living in relationship with your heavenly Father will not necessarily make you always happy. It will not answer every question, clear away every doubt, remove every obstacle. It will not mean that everything will always go right or that you will be more successful than ever before. Walking in intimacy with God is no magic formula for untold blessing. Life is still life, and life can be hard. But I can promise you that with God you will be alive as you were meant to be. Life will have the meaning it was intended to have. You will fulfill the destiny for which you were created. That is the promise of relationship with your heavenly Father."

He paused. The church was silent.

"I am going to repeat the prayer I asked you to pray," Jefferson concluded. *"I will say the words as our final prayer together. Then, in a spirit of quiet reflection, we will dismiss without a closing hymn. I hope you will pray it with me.—God,"* he said slowly and softly, *"if I am a man or woman who needs to respond to You in one of the ways spoken of this morning, please reveal it to me. Then show me what to do."*

The church was silent.

Harlowe Jefferson walked from behind the pulpit. His wife stood and joined him from the front row and together they made their way down the center aisle. Gradually the congregation rose and left the church.

It was the shortest service any of the members of Destiny Junction Community could remember. But it was also the most memorable. The clock in the narthex showed eleven minutes before noon.

Sixteen

Sally Parker left her house that same afternoon, reflecting on the church service she had attended that morning.

Something was changing within her about how she thought about God. As the words of the service replayed themselves over in her mind, she realized that Lynne Jefferson's father could not have more perfectly put into words her own misconception about the thing called salvation.

The words had struck her with such force that she had not been able to stop thinking about them since walking out of the church at noon. As it had already several times, Pastor Jefferson's voice came again into the ears of her mind.

"For many of you it may seem an old-fashioned term," he had said, *"this thing known as being 'saved.' The first question we must ask is this: Why salvation at all? What is salvation from? Obviously no one needs to be saved unless there is some kind of peril.*

"Now many would answer that question by saying we need to be saved from the fires of hell. But it has never been my view that the good news of Jesus Christ begins with fire and brimstone, especially when we look at our Lord's example. He began His own preaching with the tender words, 'Blessed are the poor in spirit, for theirs is the kingdom of heaven.'

"The fires spoken of by the prophet Malachi are real enough. Hell is no myth. But Jesus didn't start there, and neither should we. If we try to base our understanding of salvation on avoiding hell, we will never come to understand the thing properly because we will be going about it backwards.

"So I believe it is important that we begin elsewhere."

Sally saw that her mistaken image had colored everything about how she viewed the Christian message. Since the juvenile picture of the devil with horns and a tail seemed like a myth, she had dismissed the entire Christian story as irrelevant for her life right now. But could she now continue to do so?

"God," she said softly, "wherever You are and whatever You are all about, I see that I need to respond to You...not as a mythical being...not to save me from hell...but to save me from who I am *now*. I ask You to show me Your truth and reveal Yourself to me."

------◦◦◦◦------

Lidia Tolek was also out walking that Sunday afternoon thinking hard about what she had heard that morning. Like Sally Parker, words from earlier in the day reverberated inside Lidia's memory as clearly as if the pastor were right beside her.

"I ask the question again," he had said. *"What do we need to be saved from?*

"The answer I would pose is simply this—ourselves.

"Without God, we are left to ourselves—alone. Aloneness now, aloneness for eternity.

"Many, of course, do not think themselves alone. In the midst of an active, fast-paced, even happy life, it is easy to succumb to the illusion of non-aloneness."

Lidia smiled sadly to herself. She was under no illusions about her aloneness. She didn't have a single person she could really call a friend.

She wandered toward the river, paused at the water's edge, then absently kicked a few pebbles from the bank into it.

Was her life of any more lasting significance than those little stones? Would she one day disappear and never be heard from again...with no one to notice, no one to care?

Was it possible, as the minister had said, that she really *mattered* to God, that He actually *loved* her? It was too wonderful a thought to take in.

"God, if it is true," she said as she stood gazing at the flowing water, "please show me."

------◆◆◆------

Jack Snow went home from church and sat in front of the television watching football for most of the afternoon.

But he was having a difficult time keeping his mind on the game.

"You must understand that I am not speaking of mere loneliness," the pastor had said. *"This aloneness is something much different. If one is living without a daily relationship with God, then that individual is living alone, whether he or she feels loneliness or not. You may be reasonably fulfilled and contented. It doesn't matter. Without God in your heart, you are alone. It is just that simple."*

Halftime came in the late game. Snow rose and walked absently to the refrigerator for another beer. He opened the door and his eyes fell on the six-pack he was well on his way to finishing before day's end.

He hesitated, then shoved the door shut.

He didn't need another beer...he needed to think. He turned for the door and walked outside.

Why was he feeling so agitated? That service had really gotten to him. He had never thought of himself as lonely.

117

But what would those words mean if suddenly he found himself at death's door? What if he was alone after all, like the minister said—alone in that place deep inside?

Snow tried to dismiss the thought. But it would not go away. Maybe deep inside he *was* just as alone as those guys in the cells he locked up week after week.

A sobering thought.

All around town, thoughts of that morning's sermon at the Community Church was producing similar questions, reflective walks and quiet musings about life's meaning. The local football ratings, if they had been taken, would probably have registered an all-time low.

The fact was, not a few in the community of Destiny Junction that night had difficulty sleeping.

Seventeen

MONDAY, OCTOBER 27

10:12 A.M.

Almost from the moment she opened the doors of The Answer Place the next morning, Jeanne Carter found herself greeting people she had never seen in her shop before. She continued to face a constant stream of new customers for the next few days.

Most were asking for Bibles.

So frequent and similar were the requests that by two o'clock Monday, after a telephone call to Harlowe Jefferson and forty minutes in a concordance, Jeanne had printed up on the laptop computer in her office a brief list of answers to the questions she was being asked most often.

In the next few days she had to photocopy the handout repeatedly, and by week's end estimated that she had given away forty or more copies. When some of her more regular customers chanced to see it, they also asked for copies that they could give away themselves.

———◦◦◦———

Sam Gonzales walked out of The Answer Place late Monday afternoon holding the sheet of paper with Bible verses listed on it. He was not supposed to be driving so soon after the surgery, but he had wanted more information on some of the questions raised in his mind by yesterday's church service.

As he walked back to his car scanning down the page, his eyes fell on the words, *all have sinned* and underneath them, *the wages of sin is death.*

The words hit hard.

He had never thought of himself as a "sinner." But now that he was suddenly facing his own mortality, he was looking at everything in a new light. Was death indeed the result of *sin*? Or was something else involved?

Did this mean more than just death of the body? Was the death being spoken of a *spiritual* death? Were spiritual death and physical death perhaps *both* caused by this thing called sin?

Sam climbed in behind the wheel, closed the car door and read the entire sheet slowly and carefully.

Prayers suggested by Pastor Jefferson during memorial service and Sunday's sermon:

God, show me Your truth. Reveal Yourself to me. Show me my thirst and my need for You. Teach me how to live an abundant life.

God, if I am a man or woman who needs to respond to You, please reveal it to me. Then show me what to do.

Verses mentioned by Pastor Jefferson, in which Jesus says:

John 10:10—*I have come that they may have life, and have it to the full.*

John 3:3—*I tell you the truth, no one can see the kingdom of God unless he is born again.*

John 3:16—*For God so loved the world that He gave His one and only Son, that whoever believes in Him shall not perish but have eternal life.*

John 7:37—*If anyone is thirsty, let him come to Me and drink.*

Some other Bible verses about salvation:

Romans 3:23—*For all have sinned and fall short of the glory of God.*

Romans 6:23—*For the wages of sin is death, but the gift of God is eternal life in Christ Jesus our Lord.*

Romans 5:8—*God demonstrates His own love for us in this: While we were still sinners, Christ died for us.*

John 14:6—*I am the way and the truth and the life. No one comes to the Father except through me.*

John 6:35—*I am the bread of life. He who comes to Me will never go hungry, and he who believes in Me will never be thirsty.*

John 5:24—*I tell you the truth, whoever hears My word and believes Him who sent Me has eternal life.*

Romans 3:22—*Righteousness from God comes through faith in Jesus Christ to all who believe.*

John 11:25-26—*I am the resurrection and the life. He who believes in Me will live, even though he dies; and whoever lives and believes in Me will never die.*

John 1:12—*To all who received Him, to those who believed in His name, He gave the right to become children of God.*

Revelation 3:20—*Here I am! I stand at the door and knock. If anyone hears My voice and opens the door, I will go in and eat with him, and he with Me.*

1 John 5:1—*Everyone who believes that Jesus is the Christ is born of God.*

1 John 5:3—*This is love for God: to obey His commands.*

Ten minutes later Sam sat back and let out a long breath.

Now it was the second half of the same verse that was going through his mind: *the gift of God is eternal life in Christ Jesus our Lord. Eternal life.*

Suddenly the familiar words sounded strangely close and personal. Not distant. Not a mere religious phrase. All at once they seemed full of hope.

Was eternal life truly possible? The oft-used term had become powerfully relevant.

He didn't want to die. And maybe, if this was all true, there really and truly was something called eternal life...*spiritual* life.

If so...he wanted it! He didn't want this cancer to be the end for him.

He had lived his whole life putting off spiritual things. But it was high time he quit doing so. It was time he looked eternity in the face and decided what he was going to do about it.

Sam looked over the paper the bookstore lady had given to him.

There were the words in black and white: *He who believes in Me will live, even though he dies.*

But could he honestly say that he believed it?

Sam thought for a moment. Another verse came into his mind. He looked at the sheet again. Belief came by faith...*faith in Jesus Christ.*

He *would* believe them!

He would simply accept them as truth...accept them *in faith*. He would *choose* to believe.

Sam put the paper down on the car seat beside him and closed his eyes. He had never prayed aloud except to say an occasional memorized grace before a meal. This was certainly a peculiar place to begin, in the parking lot of a store. But if eternity was at hand—and for him it had never been closer—then there was no time like the present. He could never tell how many tomorrows he had left.

"God," whispered Sam Gonzales softly, "I know I haven't been much of a churchman and haven't paid enough attention to You in my life. I'm sorry about that. I guess I was just too busy getting through life to stop and think what it was all about. But things are going to be different now, for however much more time You give me. I want eternal life, and I realize from reading these verses that it's Jesus who gives it. I want to believe...no, I'm saying here and now that I do believe...I believe, like that one verse said, that Jesus is the Son of God. I'm not sure of what all that means. But I'm sure You'll help me. And I ask You to help me believe even more though I have to accept it by faith at first. If my belief is a little weak to begin with, then help it to grow stronger. And I'll try to find out more about what Jesus said, and try to start living that belief more now. I suppose I ought to get a Bible and start reading it. And I—"

He stopped, opened his eyes and picked up the sheet again. Once more he began to pray as he looked at the top of the page.

"And, God," he said, "since this is new to me and since I don't know what to do next, I want to add to my prayer what Pastor Jefferson said we ought to pray. I'd like to ask You like it says here to reveal Yourself to me and teach me how to live closer to You, and show me what You want me to do. There...I guess that's about it, so...well, amen, I guess."

He paused briefly, then glanced around, relieved that no one was staring at him in his car looking like he was talking to himself.

"Oh, and...one more thing, God," he added. "I want to say thank You for helping me like this, because I already feel better somehow. I think I will be able to face this cancer now."

Eighteen

Tuesday, October 28

7:09 A.M.

Margaret Sanderson awoke on Tuesday morning and went to the window hoping her picture-taking neighbor might be out. But she saw no one. She slipped on her robe, then put water on for a morning cup of tea.

As she sat down in her easy chair a few minutes later, Sunday's sermon stole quietly back into her memory. A few short sentences from it had repeated themselves over and over in the two days since. She knew the words had been meant for her.

"Some of you listening to me this morning perhaps are lonely," Mr. Jefferson had said. *"Your life may be a dreary existence of enduring one day after another without much human contact—real, close, personal human contact. You need God because you need companionship. You need Him because the human soul was created, not to be alone, but for fellowship with its Maker."*

By mid morning, Margaret Sanderson still sat in the chair in her living room thinking of what the pastor had said. She required no more convincing.

"God, come into my life," she prayed quietly. "I want fellowship with You just like the pastor said. I may be old and lonely, but I hope it is not too late for me to become a child. I want to know You as my Father, and I ask You to help me."

———◦◦◦———

Dixie Judd had been a little distracted all morning. The café's breakfast crowd was unusually boisterous and talkative. But Dixie wasn't in the mood. She had other things on her mind.

As soon as she'd gotten off yesterday at two, she'd gone to the Community Church to see Pastor Jefferson.

She introduced herself and told the minister about the tract Lynne had given her a year earlier.

"I'm embarrassed to tell you," she said, "that I threw it away. I guess I wasn't really too interested at the time. But after what happened…well, I am interested now. I wondered if you might have another one you could give me."

Lynne's father smiled. Every day, it seemed, he gained some new glimpse into the impact his daughter's life had invisibly had among the people of this community.

"I think so," he replied. "I have several here." He opened one of his desk drawers and pulled out a half dozen small tracts and pamphlets. He handed them across to Dixie. "Is it one of these?"

She took them and glanced through them.

"Yes…yes, this is it," she said.

"I'm glad. You may have it—and feel free to take any of the others as well."

"This one will be fine…thank you very much."

Dixie left the church, and by day's end she had read the small booklet three times.

That was yesterday. And through most of today she was still thinking about it. When it slowed down about ten and her break time came, Dixie sat down with a cup of coffee and an English muffin in the corner booth, opened her purse and took out the leaflet again. Once more she read over the now familiar words with which the leaflet began: "God loves you as personally and completely as if you were the only person on earth. *You!* And because He loves you so much, He has a wonderful and exciting plan for your life."

The two Destiny Junction journalists who were slowly being drawn into the aftermath of Lynne Jefferson's death were experiencing very different reactions to what they had heard from the pulpit on the previous Sunday.

Newspaper reporter Bertie Snow recalled the words with a certain degree of annoyance. He could not get them out of his mind.

"You see, my friends, deep down inside where no other person can go with you, in the innermost chamber of the heart, only two options exist. You are either alone, or you share that inner sanctum of the soul with your heavenly Father. No one else can go there. Not friends, parents, husband, wife, no one. Either you and God live there together, or you are by yourself. And if you are alone, it is an aloneness that will remain for all eternity."

Bertie tried to convince himself that he wasn't a bit lonely. He was busy, involved, happy and content with how things were going in his life. Hey...he was the *last* person in the world who would describe himself as alone.

Then why did he suddenly feel so—

He would not think of it anymore! He refused to think about it. It wasn't logical. A good reporter had to base what he did on logic.

He didn't need God no matter what the minister said.

Meanwhile, his television counterpart Leslie Cahill found herself quiet and introspective on Tuesday morning as she got ready to head to the station.

As she was about to walk out the door, her telephone rang.

"Is this Leslie Cahill?" said a voice she did not recognize on the other end of the line.

"Yes—that's right," she replied.

"Hello," said the voice, "…my name is Heather Fellowes."

———⊷∘⊷———

Richard Ray came into the café a little after noon. Dixie greeted him with a smile, thinking to herself that he looked tired and thin, like he hadn't been eating or sleeping too well.

"I thought you were going to that church last Sunday," he said, sitting down at the counter.

"I did."

"Where were you? I looked around."

"I don't know…halfway toward the front, I guess."

Richard shrugged.

"That's too bad," said Dixie. "I looked around for you too."

"When I didn't see you I went upstairs," said Richard.

"Where were you afterward?"

"I got right out and went back to my place."

Dixie poured him a cup of coffee.

"What do you think about it all, anyway?" he asked as he dumped some sugar in his cup, then reached for the cream.

"All what?" said Dixie.

"You know, all those religious things the guy was talking about…you know, salvation…being born again, and all that."

"I don't know—seems like there might be something to it. I've got to admit it's got me thinking."

"Yeah," nodded Richard, "me too."

He smiled and gave an odd little laugh. "Kinda weird though," he said.

"What's that?" asked Dixie.

"Me…thinking about God, religion, all that stuff."

Dixie started to go, then turned back to the counter.

"I went back again yesterday," she said.

"On Monday...what for?" asked Richard. "Aren't churches only open on Sunday?"

"Not this one. I wanted to see if I could get another copy of that thing Lynne Jefferson gave me. Didn't I tell you about it? I wanted to read it again."

"Did you get it?"

"Yep," nodded Dixie.

"Is it any good?"

"Yeah...not like anything I've ever read before, but...yeah, it's interesting. You want to read it?"

"I might."

"I'll bring it over. You might as well go ahead and take it with you. I've practically got it memorized. I can get another one."

"Right...okay, thanks, Dixie."

The waitress returned a minute later with the tract. She handed it to him, then went to tend a few other customers who had come in for lunch.

Richard sipped at his coffee as he opened the little booklet and began to read. He rose a few minutes later.

"You sure you don't mind if I borrow this?" he said as he paid for his coffee.

"No, that's fine," replied Dixie.

"All right then...I'll see you later."

Dixie watched him go, thinking to herself how lonely he must be, away from home, no family, no friends, no steady job.

But then, she thought, was her life much better?

———◆◆◆———

Stopped at a red light, Charlie Sweet saw Richard Ray leave the café and walk down the sidewalk. He watched him go, thinking how isolated the

129

fellow looked. He had seen him out walking the streets before. The kid seemed halfway clean-cut, not like most of the bums who frequented the streets day after day. What was his story, the patrolman wondered. What was he doing here in Destiny Junction?

Sweet thought about what he had heard last Sunday sitting there next to Jack Snow. If anybody ever looked like he needed what the preacher had been talking about, that kid who had just come out of the café did.

The light turned green and the patrolman eased his car forward.

But as for himself, he thought, he wasn't about to go weak in the knees and start getting religious now.

Keep the being saved stuff for the deadbeats down on Second Street who were really in bad shape, he thought.

He wasn't in any danger.

———◦◦◦———

That evening, the lead feature on the six o'clock news was the interview, taped only two hours before, between Leslie Cahill and Heather Fellowes, in which Heather had gone on camera to tell what had happened on the fateful morning of Lynne Jefferson's shooting.

When the taping had come to an end, Cahill, cameraman Lane Rakestraw and the rest of the news crew packed up their things and prepared to leave.

Heather stood as if waiting for something.

"You...expecting someone?" asked Cahill as she began walking toward her car.

"No...no, not really," replied Heather.

"You need a ride someplace? Be glad to give you a lift."

"No, I've got no place to go. I just..."

She had been going to say that she was afraid to go back to the hotel she called home, that she had nowhere to turn for help.

But she couldn't say all that. She hardly knew this lady. Why would a well-known newscaster care about the troubles of a two-bit hooker?

"No, that's okay," said Heather with a shrug. "I gotta get home, I guess...and, you know...get ready for work."

"Okay, if you're sure," said Cahill. "Thanks again for the interview. It was real brave of you."

"Hey, baby!" said Reggie Kincaid as he walked into Heather's room several hours later. "You were dynamite on the tube tonight! Hank's in trouble now that you fingered him in front of everyone!"

"Reggie, do I have to go tonight?" moaned Heather. "I'm too tired—from the interview and all. Can't you—"

"Hey, baby," interrupted the big black man, "you been taking too much time off lately. Time we got back on track."

"But, Reggie...please."

"Don't try to do Reggie wrong," he snapped. His voice was hard. "You know what happens."

Heather fought back the tears. She knew if Reggie caught her crying, he would be even harder on her. Some of the girls said he had ways of making you hurt that never showed a mark. She didn't want to find out how.

When she got home late that same night, sometime after two in the morning, she flopped down on her bed and finally broke and sobbed.

If she tried to leave, Reggie would kill her.

Who could rescue her from this horrible life she had gotten herself into?

Nineteen

3:51 P.M.

Richard Ray was walking along the waterfront that afternoon. As he went he pulled out the tract and began to read it again. Like Dixie, he had now been through it several times.

"Mankind was created to live in fellowship with God," he read, "but because of his stubborn self-will, he chose to go his own independent way. This sin caused man to be separated from God, from the time of Adam and Eve all the way to the present—right down to you and me. We are all sinners because we do not obey God."

If ever a phrase described his own attitude toward life, toward God...actually toward everything, thought Richard, that was it...*his own stubborn self-will.*

And where had his independence gotten him? Nowhere but in the middle of an empty and pointless life.

He'd never told Dixie this, but he had been raised in a religious home. He knew all this stuff. But he had always hated it...the do's and don'ts, the boring church services, being watched, the feeling that someone was going to slap your wrist if you stepped out of line.

But now for some reason the familiar words out of his past felt like a balm for his troubled spirit. He couldn't explain it, but all at once he knew he was ready to make a change.

133

Again he looked down at the tract and picked up reading where he had left off.

"Jesus Christ is the only way for man to bridge the gap that sin has created between God and man," Richard read. "His death on the cross conquered sin's power in the world and enables us, by trusting in what Christ has done, once again to enter into fellowship with God."

He continued reading through to the end.

When Richard had completed the booklet, a sense of resolve came over him. What he had been unable to do as a mixed-up and independently minded teenager, he knew he was ready to do now. He would be twenty in two months. It was time to end this decade of rebellion.

He continued until he came to one of the little grassy areas alongside the city harbor where they'd put in a few benches. He sat down and gazed out over the water of the protected bay where a hundred or more of the local fishing boats were moored.

Gradually his spirit calmed. Then Richard Ray closed his eyes and began to pray words that no one else in all the world ever heard.

"Lord," he said softly, "I'm sorry for being so stubborn. I've known for a long time that I needed to accept You as my Savior—for *me*, not because my parents and everyone at church said I should. Thank You for being patient with me. I finally see that I really need You, Jesus. I know You died on the cross for me. So I want to ask You now to come into my heart. God, thank You for forgiving my sins through Jesus' death. Take control of my life and show me what You want me to do. Help me to begin obeying You. Help me to make more out of the next ten years of my life than I have these last ten. Amen."

That same Wednesday evening, a brief replay came on the Chambers newscast of a shocking personal interview from one of the local stations a hundred miles to the north that had run on the previous evening.

Judith Fellowes was in the kitchen slicing vegetables for salad when suddenly her ears perked up. She turned toward the television in the adjacent sitting room, and the next instant her eyes shot open.

Knife and stalk of celery fell to the floor as she ran to the set shouting. "Matthew...Matthew, come quickly."

A few minutes later both sat weeping in front of the television. They wept for their prodigal daughter. They wept for what she had become. They wept with anguished thanksgiving to God for showing them at last where she was. They wept to learn that she was still so close to home.

"Oh, Matthew," said Judith as tears streamed down her face, "she doesn't look good. I hardly recognize her. I think she is in some kind of trouble. Oh, Matthew, I don't think I can bear it!"

Already the seminary professor, while wiping at his eyes with a tissue, was picking up the telephone to call the station in hopes of getting as much information as he could.

A call to Channel 3 in Destiny Junction followed. Miss Cahill, he was told, was unavailable, but he could leave his name and number. He declined, saying he would see her in person tomorrow.

The final call was to his secretary at her home.

"I don't know how long we'll be gone," he said in reply to her question. "As long as it takes. Put a notice on my door that my classes will be canceled on Thursday and Friday."

He hung up the telephone and turned back to his distraught wife.

"We'll drive to Destiny Junction first thing in the morning."

The next moment they were on their knees together, thanking God for this sudden break in the clouds after praying for a year without a hint of information about their daughter.

"Oh, God," prayed Judith, "soften dear Heather's heart toward us."

"And give us tenderness toward her," added Matthew. "Create in her a readiness to know that our hearts contain nothing but love and forgiveness."

The interview with the Fellowes girl brought the whole incident to the forefront of Lane Rakestraw's mind. When he recalled the words he had heard last Sunday about the difference between sin and sins, he had jolted straight up where he sat.

He had always considered himself to be a decent sort of guy. He'd gone to church as a kid. He always figured he was more or less a Christian. He was moral and all that. He'd never slept with anyone, never stolen anything and believed the Christian story. Life was treating him okay.

Then *bam*! The preacher's words hit him straight between the eyes.

"There is another myth perpetrated by the hellfire preachers of old that salvation is only for terrible sinners. But what is sin other than being separated from God?

"Sin is not something you do at all. It is the description of the innermost region of the heart I was talking about. If self rules in that inner sanctum, and we are going our own way, doing our own thing, then we're not one with God.

"That's sin, the conflict between self-will and God's will. Self on the throne of life, which can be either outright rebellion against God's ways or mere passive indifference toward God. But the result is the same.

"Good people are sinners just as much as bad people. Don't let your goodness fool you into thinking you need God any less than the most horrible person who ever lived."

Lane had heard the words "a personal relationship with Jesus Christ." But he'd never bothered much about it.

But that phrase out of the pastor's mouth really hit home—*passive indifference toward God.*

Wow, that was him exactly!

What a sobering thought. Even though he believed in God and Jesus, he couldn't call his "relationship" with either of them very *personal*.

Heather Fellowes didn't know if she could take one more night being one of Reggie's girls.

But what could she do? It was horrible!

As she began to get dressed, she thought about last Sunday's sermon on salvation. For so long she had tried to run from God. But the moment she heard Pastor Jefferson's words, her heart had stung like a knife slicing straight through her skin.

Whatever he said about respectability, that wasn't her. She knew she had done awful things.

"Sins, on the other hand, are what we do—bad things that contradict God's commands. If we're not walking with God, we need to repent for those sins. Christians are not immune from sins either, which is why the Christian life is not a life of perfection but one of trying, with God's help, to conquer what the Bible calls our sinful nature.

"The myth I mentioned is so damaging to an understanding of salvation because it conveys the notion that our need of salvation is based on wickedness. It implies that only very bad people, genuinely miserable sinners, need God at all.

"But the fact is, we all need Him."

She certainly needed saving if anyone did!

"God help me," Heather said softly, beginning to cry. "My life's a mess...I don't know where to turn...please... please, God, help me!"

She tried to pull herself together, then looked at the clock. Eight-thirteen. Reggie would be here any minute.

A knock came to the door. She knew the sound.

A sick feeling in Heather's stomach made her almost gag.

Reggie walked in without benefit of further invitation. The look on his face showed that he had about had it with this timid little girl.

"Reggie...Reggie, please," whimpered Heather, "I just can't do it anymore."

"Hey, babe," he replied, "I told you before, there ain't no backing out on the man." His tone was sinister, his intent clear.

He grabbed her arm sharply and began moving toward the door, which stood partially open.

"Ouch...ow," cried Heather. "Reggie—that hurts!"

"Shut up and come with me!"

Suddenly another knock sounded against the door.

Taken off guard, for an instant Reggie froze.

Another knock.

"Hello...anybody home?" came a voice.

"Get lost, man!" barked Reggie. "We're busy."

Heather looked around him, and now saw the face peering through the opening. She couldn't believe her eyes!

"Daddy!" she cried. She broke free from Reggie's grasp, ran to the door and the next moment was trembling and crying in her father's arms.

"It's all right now, Heather," whispered Matthew Fellowes, gently stroking his daughter's hair and trying to calm her.

"Hey, man, what is this!" said Reggie, walking slowly forward. "Whoever you are, this young lady's mine for the night. So I'd advise you to get out of here before you get yourself hurt."

Still holding his daughter, the seminary professor looked up toward the imposing form of the black man approaching him. He appeared to be 6'3" or 6'4", and powerful enough to do any man plenty of harm if he wanted to.

"I don't know who you are, sir," said Matthew in a calm but firm voice. "But this is my daughter, and in the name of the Lord Jesus I tell you that you will not lay another hand on her.—Heather, dear," he said, speaking softly while he kept his eyes locked on Reggie's, "your mother is downstairs waiting. Go down to her...I will be all right."

Heather slipped from his arms and ran for the stairs.

"I am going to tell you again," said her father, "my daughter is through with you. Now I am going to walk down these stairs and you are not going to do anything except leave peaceably after we are gone. Heather is coming with us."

Matthew Fellowes turned and followed Heather down the stairs, where his wife and daughter were by now in tearful reunion.

Behind him, Reggie Kincaid stood in silence. He was stunned as much by the sudden turn of events as by his own inaction to do anything but watch helplessly while the honky ordered him around.

Twenty

Bruce Penley shuffled nervously toward the door of Destiny Junction Community Church, hesitated one last time, then opened it and walked inside.

"I'd like to see the reverend, if you don't mind, ma'am," he said to the secretary when he had located the office.

"I'll see if he is available," she replied, bracing herself against the pungent odor that had followed the man through the door. "And your name?"

"Penley, ma'am...Bruce Penley. But he don't know me."

Two minutes later the scruffy homeless man was seated in Pastor Jefferson's office.

"I'm obliged to you for taking the time to see me," Penley began. "I knew your daughter...well, in a way, you might say. She give me a Bible and was always mighty nice to me. I'm real sorry about what happened, Reverend."

"Thank you, Mr. Penley," nodded the minister.

Penley chuckled. "Ain't nobody calls me mister, reverend," he said. "But why I came is that I was in your service last week, 'cause I was real fond of your daughter. And after listening to you, I figured if ever a fellow was in trouble, you might be the kind of man who might give him a hand, that is, if you're anything like your daughter, which I figure you must be.

141

And you see, the thing is, reverend, that I ain't been doing too good these last few years, but…well, with your girl giving me that Bible, and then with them things you was saying about a fellow trying to get his life right with God and all…you see, reverend, I'd like to try to start making something of myself. I know it's a mite late, but I figure I been sponging off the system too long and doing nobody no good. So what I came to ask is if you might know somewhere a run-down old fellow like me might get a little work to make a start of turning his life around. I ain't looking for no handout from the church collection plate, but some good honest labor. I can work, reverend, and, well…for the first time in a long while I *want* to work."

"I am delighted to hear of your resolve, Mr. Penley," replied Jefferson. "The first step out of any trouble is the decision to take a step in the right direction. And that first step is the most important. I have every confidence that you will make rapid progress. And I just may have an idea for you. There is a man in our congregation, one of our respected members. It just may be that he might have some temporary work at one of his job sites. I'll write his name down for you. In fact," he added as he took out a pen and began to write on a notepad, "I will call him and tell him to expect you."

"I'm more obliged than I can tell you, reverend," replied Penley enthusiastically. "That's real kind of you."

"I am happy to help," said Harlowe Jefferson. "Here's his name and address—it's Kingston Construction."

———⌖———

Yvonne Seymour stood in front of her locker between second and third period on Thursday morning. It was starting to bug her that after four days she could still not stop thinking about that church service.

Yvonne could still hear Mr. Jefferson's question, followed by the astonishing answer. It had taken her all this time to try to absorb his words.

"Let's be honest, very few of us really do consider ourselves quite that bad. Those of you listening right now—do you honestly consider yourselves sinners?"

She glanced down the hall. A crowd of girls was headed this way and would be clustered around her within a few seconds. Half a dozen guys would ask her out at lunch hour if they thought they could get away with it with Brock. She was one of the most popular girls in this whole school.

Why was she thinking about all this religious stuff all of a sudden?

————◦◦◦————

Around the church that Sunday morning, among staunch church members and visitors alike, Harlowe Jefferson's next words had jolted dozens of men and women upright where they sat. Scott Peyton was one of many in the community who was being goaded and plagued as he reflected on them four days later.

"That's the trouble with the 'wicked sinner' myth—most of us deep down inside consider ourselves to be pretty decent, respectable people, certainly as good as the person sitting next to you in the pew, or the guy down the street. So what do we need God for? It's easy to shrug the whole thing off."

Peyton had built the local Farmer's Fund insurance franchise into the largest single carrier in the region, and had made him a wealthy man in the process. He was doing well and was proud of it. His devilishly good looks and winning personality did nothing to dampen his inflated self-image.

Raised a Catholic, Peyton flattered himself that he was a believing Christian, which, in his lexicon of values meant that he was just as religious as he needed to be, but not an inch more. Unfortunately that little bit of "religion" had not been enough, as it were, to leaven the whole lump. He was as carnal as they came, and his loose tongue indicated clearly enough that he did not hold the name of the Lord in as high esteem even as his own. Mass on Sundays, business from Monday through Friday, and golf on Saturdays—that was how he saw his life. Give God His due, just make sure that lip service didn't exceed a respectable three percent of his time and perhaps one percent of his bank account. As to a personal and daily walk of obedience to the Scriptures, he hadn't so much as a clue that such things ought to be involved in a man's life.

But Peyton carried a healthy insurance policy on Destiny Junction Community Church, and thus he felt it his duty to be seen at the memorial service for the daughter of its pastor. What exactly had compelled him to leave Sunday's Mass the following Sunday, drive across town, and take in the eleven o'clock service at the Community Church as well, he couldn't have said. But whatever the reason, ever since the pastor's words had been sticking with him every moment.

For the first time in his life, he had begun to think about what kind of person he was. And his reflections were not that pleasant.

Even more important, he found himself wondering about what kind of person he wanted to be.

———◦❖◦———

Dr. Sarah Woo had been stirred up enough at the memorial service. But on the following Sunday the words, "as good as the person sitting next to you in the pew," caught strangely in her brain.

Unconsciously she had glanced to her right. She didn't know the lady beside her, but Rev. Jefferson's words triggered a quick chain reaction within her. Did she in fact consider herself just a little better than everyone else?

"Well, I'll tell you what we need God for. We need Him not because we're so bad—which we all are to varying degrees. Some of us are better, some of us are worse, than others. We need Him because, if we haven't

invited Him into our hearts, we're all alone in that innermost place deep inside our souls."

Did her prestige in the community as a respected physician mean that she didn't have the same spiritual needs as everyone else?

All at once Sarah Woo wasn't sure. Had she been using her respectability as an excuse to ignore God? People talked about God being a crutch. Perhaps she had been using her respectability and intelligence as crutches.

Like many others present the previous Sunday, Dr. Woo found herself saying the words along with the minister at the end of the service, "God, if I need to respond to You in some way this morning, please reveal it to me, and then show me what to do."

She hadn't even thought about it at the time. The mood was quiet and reverent, and she just found herself saying them along with Rev. Jefferson, as much out of respect for him as anything else.

Ever since, her brain had been in overdrive. Maybe God *was* showing her.

———⊷◦◦◦⊶———

All around town that Thursday, many others who had listened to the salvation sermon on Sunday, all seemingly respectable and self-assured members of the community, four days later were still trying to come to terms with their own misconceptions of what the minister had called the wicked sinner myth. Many of these were respectable men and women who had never considered religion to be necessary for successful men and women like themselves. Suddenly that notion was being turned upside down with this incredible idea that the need for salvation was not based on success, wealth, respectability, intelligence, happiness or even goodness in the world's eyes...but was a *universal* need shared by all.

That the content of a sermon could have been a subject that so many in town were thinking about might seem incredible, especially a sermon on

145

salvation. But strange vibrations had been set in motion by Lynne Jefferson's death. Everyone, it seemed, was affected, and no one was able to slow the gathering momentum of the collective conscience of the community.

Salvation was coming to this small town, and the still small voice continued to speak.

Leslie Cahill was one of those still wrestling with the content of the sermon, though not by choice. She had the feeling she was being hauled before the court of truth against her will.

The interview with Heather Fellowes brought to the surface her varied reactions during the previous Sunday's service. And now the words of the sermon repeated themselves over and over in her memory. She had never before considered the idea that sin was not what you *did*—whether you were good or bad—but the state of your existence.

From this standpoint, a happy, decently good and successful person was just as much a sinner as a criminal on death row.

What a revolutionary idea!

Was *she* just as much a "sinner" as Hank Dolan?

Whoa—she didn't quite know how to deal with that one!

If it was true, that would be a news scoop! *Everyone* needed God.

She wondered if the program director would want to lead on the evening news with *that*!

"We need saving from our separation. We need God, not necessarily because we are going around committing heinous crimes from morning till night, but because we're supposed to share life with Him.

"So you see, we're all sinners together—decent people, mean people, good people, bad people—until we let God into our hearts. I repeat—we're all sinners together...and we need God."

If this was true, thought Leslie, then that "everyone" must include her. Respectable pillar of the community whose face everyone saw each evening with her respectable smile—she needed God too.

"Tom, hello—it's Harlowe Jefferson," came the voice on the telephone when the contractor answered it, "…at the church."

"Oh…oh, yes, hello Rev. Jefferson," replied Tom Kingston. Immediately he began to perspire. "Uh…what can I do for you?" he asked.

With his conscience doing double duty against him, hearing the minister's voice on the other end of the line was almost like God Himself knocking him on the head to say, "You're not fooling anyone, Tom Kingston—I'm watching every move you make!"

"Tom, I've got a favor to ask," said Jefferson, unaware of the other's nervousness. "A fellow just came to see me, a homeless man. He's looking for work and something told me we needed to reach out to him. I wouldn't call you unless I thought it was a special case. I don't know if you've got anything or not, but if you could put him on for a week I'd appreciate it. Maybe he'll work out for you, maybe he won't. If not, the church will pick up the tab for a week's wages."

"That's hardly a proposition I could object to," laughed Tom, relieved to find out the nature of the call. "Sure, I'd be glad to."

"Good—I already gave him your name and address. His name's Penley."

"We're framing in a couple of houses. I'll give him a hammer and put him to work."

"That should help him get on his feet at least," said the pastor. "Thanks, Tom, I knew I could count on you. We'll have to get together for lunch sometime."

"Uh, yeah…right. You bet…anytime."

"Thanks again."

Doug Taggart was not as shocked by his reaction to the whole thing as some of the other people in town. Taggart was a logical man, and he tried to formulate a logical response.

He had gone to the memorial service and attended church the following morning out of respect for the Jeffersons. Logic notwithstanding, however, he hadn't expected it to set off such inner reflection. And now as he prepared for Friday's press conference to announce the bank merger, he couldn't get Jefferson's words out of his mind.

"The conclusion, therefore, may shock many of you when I say it. If you are not living in daily relationship with God, then you need salvation just as much as the man down in the county jail right now who is accused of shooting my daughter. You, my friend.

"Salvation does not save us just from being bad. Nor does it automatically make us good. Christians have a difficult time obeying God's principles just like everyone else. I want to make it very clear that salvation is not primarily about badness and goodness. It is about the difference between aloneness and relationship.

"We all need God in our hearts. He intended to live in daily relationship with the men and women He created."

Taggart glanced down again at the papers on his desk. But it was no use. He had to get this settled once and for all.

He reached for his telephone book.

"Hello...Rev. Jefferson—it's Doug Taggart," he said a few moments later, "...right, over at the bank."

He paused momentarily to listen.

"No, nothing about your car loan—it's personal. I wondered if I might make an appointment to see you sometime?"

Another pause.

"I'm awfully tied up the rest of today and tomorrow…any chance you'd have half an hour on Saturday…oh, great—thank you. I appreciate it…right, I'll see you then."

———◆———

Tom Kingston walked back to the construction site from the trailer where he had taken the call from Harlowe Jefferson.

How much longer, he wondered, could he stall the creditors? He was expecting the repo man any day.

How much longer could he stall Michelle? She was none too pleased with his sudden coolness. If he didn't give her a good explanation, it would be just like her to squawk and make a fuss.

And what about Barbara? He had a bad feeling she might know something.

How much longer could he stall Harlowe Jefferson, whose voice on the telephone sent his thoughts back to the previous Sunday.

"In very simplified terms, then," the pastor had said as Tom sat there with his family, *"that's what salvation is—living in relationship with God. You need this relationship because it is how you were made to live. Without it, life will never be entirely right."*

Tom walked to the portable bathroom, went inside and locked the door. His face was burning and he was having trouble blinking back the tears. He turned on the trickle of water from the small tank above the plastic wash basin and splashed cold water on his face.

Tom knew he was a sinner. Pillar in the church though his parents had been, his own status was clear enough by now.

Maybe the question he should be asking himself was…how much longer could he stall God?

149

———◆◈◈◆———

Heather Fellowes awoke.

Groggily she turned over in her bed. She had been sleeping on and off all day. This must have been the third or fourth nap she had taken.

What time was it?

She looked at the clock. Three-thirty in the afternoon.

The hours since her father and mother had come for her had passed like a dream. The quiet drive home to Chambers, she relaxing with her mother's arm around her like when she was a girl...dozing off occasionally...a few tears, but not many words.

They arrived back home in the city about eleven...a bath...clean clothes, then to bed in her own room...the room she hadn't seen in a year.

Then today...breakfast...back to bed...emotional exhaustion sapping every ounce of strength and causing her to sleep like she hadn't slept in months. She had hardly spoken all day. Her father and mother were being so kind...so full of tender love. Not a word of reproach...only smiles, hugs, gracious ministration. How could she have ever thought them otherwise? They were just the same as always—she recognized every gesture, every kindness. She had once found the atmosphere in this home so stifling. Now it was an oasis of peace such as she had not let herself imagine she would ever know again. How could she have had everything so wrong.

As she lay in bed, words from last Sunday's sermon in Destiny Junction gradually filtered into her brain, as if strangely mingling her recent past life with the *now* of her homecoming. She could hear Rev. Jefferson's words as clearly as if he was right beside her.

"You've all heard the word gospel. But do you know what it means?

"Gospel means good news.

"Now, what is this good news? It is that God not only can save us from our aloneness, but that He also loves us, wants the best for us, has a fulfilling

150

plan for each of our lives. He wants us to be content, full of joy and fully alive to all life has to offer. He wants to shower His love upon us and give us a rich and abundant life.

"In short, God is our Father. That's what Jesus said. A good and loving Father who wants the very best for us.

"That is good news! That's what life with God is—a relationship with a heavenly Father who is dedicated to bring about good in our lives to the extent we trust Him to do so."

Heather lay a few more minutes, gradually coming more and more to herself. For the first time all day she began to feel truly rested...and hungry.

A life of joy...an abundant life. It sounded too good to be true! Could she ever know such a life after what she had done?

A good and loving father...

She had just such a father, thought Heather—a good man, a godly man, a giving and unselfish man.

How could she not have seen it! She had been given the best parents in the world...and yet had thrown that relationship away.

She drew in a deep breath. Well, she was home now. The nightmare was over.

She rose and got dressed. It was time she did what she knew she had to do. She would not shirk or avoid it. At last she was ready. She *wanted* to do it.

She walked into the kitchen where her mother and father were both seated.

"Hello, dear," said Judith, standing and embracing her in a warm hug, "how are you feeling?"

"Better, Mother," replied Heather, returning the embrace affectionately. "Much better. I finally feel rested. And my appetite is coming back."

"Good...what would you like to eat?"

"Nothing just yet, Mother," replied Heather, stepping back and sitting down at the table. "I want to say something first."

Her mother returned to her chair.

"Mother…Daddy," began Heather, looking at both her parents in turn, "I don't know what to say other than to tell you how sorry I am. I don't know how you ever could, but I want to ask you to forgive me for all the horrible things I said and did, and most of all for doubting you. I could have trusted you…I *should* have trusted you. I will regret it all my life."

"Oh, dear," said Judith, beginning to cry, "of course we forgive you."

"I know that, Mother. I think I finally realize how much you love me."

She glanced toward her father and tried to smile.

"Oh, Daddy…I am so sorry!"

She broke down in tears. The next minute Matthew was at her side. She stood and melted into his loving arms. They stood at least a minute in silence, father weeping as freely as mother and daughter.

At last Heather stepped back and wiped at her eyes.

"I know you both forgive me," she said. "I know you accept me and love me. My eyes are now open to so many things I could not see before. But—"

She hesitated.

"What is it, dear?" said Matthew. "You may say anything without fear. We will not—"

"I know, Daddy. That's not what I was thinking. It's just…you have to realize—this is hard, but it's something I know I need to do…something I want to do. What I realize is that I need to start over, not just with the two of you, and I suppose with myself too…but most of all I need to start over with the Lord."

Again Judith Fellowes began to softly cry. She had not dared dream for such a day. Now suddenly here it was.

"What I want to ask, Daddy," Heather continued, "is if you would pray with me and help me give my heart to the Lord. I know I went forward when

I was twelve and was baptized. But it didn't mean anything then. I don't know if I'm a Christian at all, and I want to be sure. Would you do that with me, Daddy?"

"Of course, dear," replied Matthew tenderly. "Nothing could make us happier than to pray with you."

"Can we do it right now?" said Heather. "I've wasted enough time...I don't want to wait a minute longer to turn my life around."

Matthew sat back down. The three drew their chairs together, then mother, father and daughter joined hands. It was not the first time their hands had rested together in a circle. But henceforth the threefold cord of love between them would last till all eternity.

"Our Lord and Father," Matthew began after several seconds of silence, "we all come to You with grateful hearts. We thank You for bringing Heather home, for being with her during her time away, and for creating in her heart a hunger to live in fellowship with You. We pray, Lord, that You would richly satisfy that desire, and draw her closer and closer to You all the days of her life."

He fell silent. A few sniffles could be heard. The next voice to be heard was Heather's. It was all the father could do to keep from breaking into sobs of rejoicing as he listened.

"Dear Jesus," said Heather softly, "I am so sorry for going my own way, for being so rebellious and independent, and for hurting Mother and Daddy. I ask Your forgiveness for the horrible things I've done. I know You and God love me too, just like they do, and I thank You that You never stopped loving me even when I wasn't listening. I don't know if I was a Christian before. Even if I was I'm sure I forced You out of my life a long time ago. So I want to invite You back into my heart now, Jesus. I receive You as my Savior, and I thank You for dying on the cross for my sins. But I also now want to make You Lord of my life. Please help me. I want to live for You from now on. But I have so much to learn. I give my whole self to You, and ask You to use me somehow, even though up till now my life hasn't been good for very much. Take me, Lord...use me...and help me to live for You."

By now Heather was freely weeping, great tears of release and relinquishment streaming down her cheeks. The soft *amen* that next sounded from her lips was nearly inaudible. It could barely be heard, except by the angels who were rejoicing in heaven at the one lost sheep that at last had come home.

Twenty-one

FRIDAY, OCTOBER 31

7:13 A.M.

Brock Yates had been a little quiet all week.

He knew Yvonne thought something was wrong. Maybe something was wrong. But he couldn't deny that he felt different after last Sunday... strange...thoughtful.

It wasn't like him, but that sermon had really gotten to him. Yvonne thought the whole thing was ridiculous. But Brock wasn't sure. He found himself noticing things all week, looking at people differently, wondering which of the kids walking in the halls might be Christians, who believed in God, who didn't.

He'd even prayed a couple of times.

Now that was weird! BMOC Brock Yates, homecoming king, hero of the big game...man, if anybody found out about this stuff!

What in the heck was going on, anyway?

Brock walked onto the campus of Destiny Junction High a little after seven on Friday morning. The football season was coming down to a close and a league championship was on the line. Every extra hour he could get in the weight room or in going over the playbook might be the thing that would make the difference. This morning he came in early because he wanted to review tonight's game plan and the two new plays the coach had put in this week.

It was a quiet morning. Not too many people were around yet. As he approached the gym, Brock heard something that sounded like it had come from behind the side wall. It seemed metallic...a repetitive clicking. He recognized it. And he knew the ROTC class wasn't here this early!

A chill swept through him.

Brock ran to the side of the building. The instant he rounded the corner, a figure in a long black coat turned to run. Instinctively, Brock gave chase.

"Hey!" he called, sprinting after him. "Hey, come back here."

The other was running awkwardly. Brock quickly caught up. By now he had a suspicion who it was.

"Tolek...hey, man—hold up," he called again. "What's going on?"

Realizing it was no use, the cloaked figure slowed, then stopped, keeping the heavy coat pulled across the front of his body.

"How'd you know who I was?" he said testily as he turned around.

"I recognized you," said Brock. "What's going on—what are you doing?"

"Nothing's going on," said Trent. "Just mind your own business, Yates."

"What you got under your coat?"

"Nothing. What's it to you!"

"I thought I heard something a minute ago...something I didn't like."

"Aw...leave me alone." Trent turned and began to walk off.

"Tolek, come on, man," said Brock, "if it's nothing, let me take a look. Then I'll pretend I never saw you."

He took a couple of steps after him, reaching out and placing a hand on Trent's shoulder to restrain him. "Let me see what's inside your coat."

Trent squirmed away, then spun around, hatred in his eyes. As he did, one of the flaps of the coat flew open. He grabbed to pull it back. But it was too late.

"Tolek! How'd you get a rifle in here? Come on, man—this is crazy!"

"Get away from me, Yates!" Trent cried. Slowly he began to back up. "Get away, I tell you, or I'll shoot you first!"

"Don't be crazy, man," said Brock. "Don't turn our school into another massacre."

"And why not—what's this place ever done for me?"

"You'll go to jail for the rest of—"

"Yeah, and what do you care what happens to me!"

As he spoke, Trent pulled out the semi-automatic, whose bits and pieces he had been smuggling onto the grounds for weeks. He pointed it straight at the football star.

"I got my reasons," he said. "And maybe I don't plan to be around long enough for them to put me in jail. Everybody else is getting famous around here, so now I figure maybe it's my turn. And I might as well begin right now with—"

Suddenly Brock rushed him.

The dash came unexpectedly and with as much force as if Trent had been an opposing defensive line. He stumbled back, dropped the rifle and fell. Trying to recover himself, he scrambled on his knees toward it. But a kick from Brock's foot sent the weapon out of reach. The next instant Brock's 165-pound bulk came crashing down on top of Trent's 135-pound frame. Trent kicked and lashed out, delivering one accidental blow to his attacker's face before Brock pinned him helplessly to the ground.

"Look, Tolek—calm down," said Brock, struggling to contain him.

"I'll take you out along with everyone else!"

"You're not going to kill anybody. Come on—settle down. We can work this out."

"Yeah, right! Work it out, how?!"

"I don't know, we'll talk. You can tell me what's on your mind. I'll help."

"You...help! Right. Since when have the likes of you cared about me!"

The words stung Brock's conscience. He was silent a few seconds. Gradually Trent seemed to calm down. Brock now eased off him and slowly stood.

"Maybe you're right, Trent," said the football star. "Maybe I haven't cared. I'm sorry."

Where he lay on his back in the dirt, the last thing Trent Tolek had expected was an apology. He climbed slowly to his feet. His eyes darted back and forth. He seemed to be considering his options either in regaining control of the gun or else making a dash for it. But where could he run? If he went home, they'd just come after him. He began to realize that Brock Yates, as much as he thought he had always hated him, held his fate in his hands.

"You gonna rat on me?" he said.

"I don't know," said Brock, walking over and picking up the rifle. "I'll have to think about what's best. First thing, we're going to disassemble this gun before anyone gets hurt. I'll put it in my locker in the gym. Nobody'll see it. Then you and I are going to sit down and have a talk."

<hr>

The night before, as Heather Fellowes was riding back to Chambers with her parents, and while Trent Tolek was making last-minute plans for the shooting spree that would make him famous, Jill Chin had been sitting alone in her bedroom thinking. The events of the last two weeks had finally risen to a climax, and she knew she had to do something about them. If she was a Christian she knew there was something missing at the foundation of her walk.

Who was she trying to kid—she didn't even have a "walk" of faith. She had grown up in the church but had never paid any attention to what it actually *meant* to be a Christian. She believed the right things. But all that meant was what she had been taught to believe.

Had she ever actually made Jesus *Lord* of her life? Had she ever really tried to *live* her Christianity? Had she ever done one single thing because God told her to?

Jill knew the answer to all three questions was no.

But now...with everything that had happened...maybe she was finally ready to get serious about her faith.

"Lord," she prayed, "if I need to respond to You, like Rev. Jefferson said, please show me what to do."

Almost immediately, the words of the sermon came back to her.

"How, then, does one enter into that relationship of intimacy I have been talking about, and begin living the abundant life?

"That is why God sent Jesus to the earth, to live among us as a man though He was also God's Son—to tell us and show us how to do this incredible thing. This is not the time for me to try to outline the specifics of that life. That is the point of studying the Gospels, to learn from Jesus' own mouth just what life with God is like. If you want to know more, the Sermon on the Mount of Matthew 5-7 is an excellent place to begin. This morning, however, I want us to focus our attention on how salvation begins."

Immediately Jill reached for her Bible, opened it to Matthew 5, and began reading. Twenty minutes later she put it down.

"Dear Jesus, thank You," she said. "I want to make You Lord of my life. I commit myself in a new way to You. Help me to live these principles more personally. Help me really begin *practicing* the life we're supposed to live."

And now today, on Friday, for the first time ever, Jill had brought her Bible to school. She was ready to get earnest about being a Christian. She intended to read the Sermon on the Mount over again at lunch. If she meant business about this, she had to try to find practical ways to start *doing* what Jesus said.

———◆◈◈◆———

Between fifth and sixth period, Brock Yates saw Trent Tolek walking along the hall in the science wing. He hurried ahead to catch up.

"Hey, man," said Brock as he drew alongside, "how's it going...you okay?"

"I don't know...yeah, I guess," shrugged Trent. "What are you going to do? I ain't seen any cops coming for me yet."

"I didn't tell anyone," said Brock. "I thought maybe I'd come over to your place tomorrow and we could talk. Maybe we'll get rid of the thing together. The gym'll be open on Saturday. I think we could sneak it out."

"What do you mean...get *rid* of it?"

"I don't know, take it apart...throw it in the river or something."

"You'd do that for me...just get rid of the evidence?"

"I don't know...we'll see. But you'd have to promise me this is the end of it. Otherwise, you know...I'd have no choice but to tell."

"Yeah, I know," shrugged Trent.

He slowed. "Here's my class," the junior said.

"You coming to the game?" asked Brock.

"I'm not interested in sports much."

"Why don't you come tonight? Then afterward you and I can go get a hamburger or something."

"You and me...right. And how many other hundred people?"

"No, just you and me. What do you think—you want to?"

"Maybe...yeah, okay."

"Come to the locker room as soon as the game's over," said Brock. "I'll take a quick shower, then we'll split."

"I thought there was a dance."

"I don't care about it."

"What about...you know, don't you have a girlfriend?"

"She'll be okay."

"All right, then...guess I'll see you tonight."

———————

The last thing Carole Laudine had ever considered in relation to herself was being born again. The thing was ridiculous. She didn't even believe in God! Or...so she'd always thought.

Was it possible she believed in Him more than she wanted to admit?

Pangs of conscience were not something she was used to. She had gone to the memorial service out of respect for Lynne Jefferson—and because of the guilt she felt for being condescending toward her.

But why had she gone back on the following Sunday? A skeptic like her? She still wasn't sure. She was as confused about her own thought processes during these last two weeks as she was about what she really did believe.

But she couldn't make the words of Mr. Jefferson go away.

"Jesus called this change from non-relationship with God into relationship with Him being born again.

"Think about those words, my friends. Born again! No wonder Nicodemus was astonished at what Jesus told him. To be born again involves a major change in life. Inviting the Spirit of God into residence in the heart where till now we have done whatever we wanted, calling no one Lord or Master—it is as significant a moment as birth."

Carole Laudine was not in the habit of thinking anyone had a right to be over her or tell her what to do. This was the 21st century, and she was an independent, liberated woman.

Born again!

She needed no *lord* in her life!

———————

Having no idea that her brother had gone to school that day planning to commit mass murder, then be killed himself in a wild shoot-out with the police, Lidia Tolek walked slowly home that Friday afternoon thinking about many things.

Only five days ago she had prayed that God would show her if she really did matter to Him. All week she had felt strangely happy inside. Had He actually answered her prayer?

In her mind today were more words she had heard in church the previous Sunday.

"It truly is a second birth, for when God takes up residence within us, not only are we no longer alone, but we also are no longer in charge. God now becomes our Father, and as such we place ourselves in relationship with Him as His child."

Instead of going straight home, Lidia walked down toward the river, then slowly along its bank.

She wanted to do it. She wanted to ask God into her life like the preacher said.

But something inside her was afraid. Afraid of being let down, afraid everything he said wouldn't work for her. She had never known anyone who hadn't let her down eventually. She didn't even know what a father was like.

Why would God be any different?

She sat down on a log, hardly noticing that it was wet. She would just have to trust that God was different.

Her thoughts quieted. She gazed out over the slowly moving current. Finally she closed her eyes.

"God, I'm a little nervous," she began to say aloud. "I want You in my life. I want to be a Christian. I want to know Jesus better. But it's all so new to me..."

She paused, struggling one final time with her doubts.

"I want to invite You into my heart," she continued. "Thank You for answering my prayer, if that's what You did. Thank You for making me feel that I matter to You. Please come in...and live in my heart with me. I'll be Your daughter if You'll show me how. And God...thank You for loving me."

Again she was silent. A few seconds later she opened her eyes. For the first time she realized that she was crying. The river was still moving silently past her. Everything looked the same. But somehow Lidia Tolek knew that nothing would ever be the same again. She sensed that she had crossed a divide in her life, and that she would never go back to how things were before.

She sat for another twenty minutes.

Gradually Lidia began to realize that she felt good...quiet...at peace.

Maybe what she had done wouldn't answer every question, resolve every doubt or make every problem in her life disappear. She might even still be lonely. But she knew she wouldn't be *alone* anymore.

But she was glad she had done it. She knew that God loved her.

Finally she rose, turned up the bank and began the walk home. As she went, the hint of a smile occasionally came to her lips.

She now had a Friend...and He lived in her heart.

———◈———

Jim Franklin had been a Christian of sorts for years.

But he was beginning to wonder what that meant. Lynne's death had rocked the very foundations of his belief.

He knew he was saved, knew that Jesus was his Savior. But he now realized just as clearly that he had never made Jesus his Lord. He had kept the throne of his life reserved for himself...only himself. And Pastor Jefferson's sermon the previous Sunday had stripped bare the sham of his walk with God.

"When I talk about the distinction between aloneness and relationship, make no mistake, it is not an equal sort of buddy-buddy relationship with God. There is a Father and there is a child. And the Father sets the rules.

That's why, as I said before, once we enter into this relationship, if we are serious about it, we do become better people, because within this relationship we are under obligation to obey our Father and live as Jesus taught. Jesus Himself becomes our Savior, the messenger or agent of our salvation, and also our Lord.

"That means we must do as He says.

"And Jesus has made clear very specific guidelines about how we are to conduct ourselves and about the attitudes and priorities we are to adopt.

"Walking in relationship with God, therefore, means living according to His principles. That's how the relationship works. It involves a significant shift, a change of management in life. That's why Jesus defined it with words of such enormous magnitude."

Suddenly the stark truth slammed home. Jim Franklin realized he had been playing at the "God thing," hiding behind a facade of Christian busyness. Nobody was more active than he, attending three or more worship services a week, along with Bible studies and prayer meetings seemingly on a daily basis, and being involved at the rescue mission and several other ministries. He was in The Answer Place at least once a week buying things to give away.

But it was all on his own terms.

Did that explain why there hadn't been much visible growth toward spiritual maturity, why he was still stuck on the Christian fundamentals, why nobody sought him for positions of leadership and responsibility, why he bounced from counselor to counselor, from church to church?

He had never, as the pastor had called it, made the "change of management" in his life. He had accepted Christ years ago...but he had never truly given Him his heart. Is that why he was always questioning whether he was really saved?

"Oh, Lord," Jim prayed. "I repent of having held back for so long the innermost part of my heart from You. Forgive me. Though on the surface I have maintained a facade of religiosity, I have not let You work in my life. But I want now to relinquish control. I want You to be, not only my Savior, but also my Lord. Help me, Jesus...I will need it, for I am not very experienced at denying myself. But if You will probe me and remind me when I am beginning to seize the throne again, I will do my best to yield control to You. Thank You, Lord, for showing me the true state of my life, even though it took dear Lynne's death to wake me up. And I pray for Rev. Jefferson and Anne, Lord. Be especially close to them during this time of anguish and loss."

Twenty-two

SATURDAY, NOVEMBER 1

11:45 A.M.

"I'll get right to it, Rev. Jefferson," began Taggart when the two men were seated comfortably. "I am a businessman—and a successful one. I like to think one of the reasons for my success is decisiveness. I can make decisions. Not every decision I make turns out good. But I would rather move forward and take the good along with the bad than sit idly by, afraid of launching out."

"A sound policy," smiled Jefferson.

"I also like to think that I am a man who knows a good thing when it comes along," the successful black banker went on, "and is not afraid to take a certain risk."

"I listened to your announcement of the bank merger on last evening's news," said the pastor. "You certainly have made some lucrative decisions. Congratulations."

"Thank you. Yes, the bank is doing very well. But I have to tell you, your sermon of a week ago got under my skin. I am finding myself wondering if this might just be one of those things to come along that I need to be decisive about. If the policy is sound for business, it must be equally sound in spiritual matters."

"Well put," rejoined Jefferson.

"Exactly why I asked to see you. I want to know more about what it means to be a Christian. Not the churchy variety. I've been playing that game for years so that I would look respectable. No, I mean the sort of thing you were talking about last Sunday—the kind of relationship with God you said we were made for, the kind of thing that gives a man something to live for."

"Quite a request—asking a pastor for more information on salvation."

"More than just information," said Taggart. "Tell me *why* I should dedicate myself to such a life. I'm ready and eager to listen. I make business decisions on the basis of facts. I figure I ought to do the same here. You came to me to ask about a car loan because that's *my* business. Now I'm coming to *you* asking about salvation because I assume you know more about it than I."

Taggart stopped and sat waiting.

"I have to tell you, Mr. Taggart," replied Jefferson after a moment, "that this is probably the most unusual thing I've ever been asked in my years in the pastorate. One would think people would ask ministers about salvation all the time. But it is actually very rare."

"Take your time," said Taggart. "I'm in no hurry. Tell me about yourself, if that would be easier. Why are you so in earnest about your Christianity? Tell me exactly what comprises your Christian life on a day-to-day basis. How do you actually *live* in personal fellowship with God? I am eager to know all I can. When a new investment opportunity comes along, this is what I do—I investigate the details, the facts, the pros and cons. Then I make a decision."

Jefferson thought for a few moments.

"I think I would start out," he began, "by saying that it is a life in which I choose to make God part of all I do and think. In other words, I bring Him into all my affairs, large and small. I do so for two reasons. First, to find out what is His perspective, so that I will be ordering my thoughts and decisions and attitudes according to *His* ways rather than my *own*. And secondly, I do so in order to find out what He wants me to do."

"What...*He* wants you to do?"

Jefferson nodded. "The purpose of my life is to do *God's* will rather than my own. Perhaps that is the difference, as you mentioned, between a churchy Christian and a moment-by-moment disciple and follower of Jesus Christ—bringing Him into every aspect of life. Does that make sense?"

"I think so," replied Taggart. "But I must admit the concept is foreign to everything I am accustomed to. Is not the creed of modern existence to make our *own* decisions and to do our own will?"

"You have hit the nail on the head," rejoined Jefferson. "You've exactly stated why a daily walk with God is 180 degrees at odds with, as you call it, the creed of modern existence."

"Go on...please tell me more," said Taggart eagerly. "I am very intrigued."

Twenty minutes later, having been prompted as he went by an occasional question or comment from his listener, Harlowe Jefferson at last drew his comments to a close.

"I don't know whether all that helps," he said. "But at least you now have my thorough perspective on what Christianity is all about."

"Most helpful," replied Taggart. "And it makes perfect sense. I realize there is much I still have to learn. But I know this much—I *would* like to enter into this fellowship with God you have told me about. It is clear to me that it is the right thing to do, and the only logical course of action for a thinking person to follow. What must I do?"

"Simply talk to God, tell Him what is in your heart, then express to Him your desire to yield your life to Him and become His follower."

"Would you pray with me?"

"It would be my honor."

"I must tell you, however, that I feel no great emotion."

"The emotional component of salvation is greatly exaggerated," rejoined Jefferson. "Some teach that emotion is always involved. But this is inaccurate. One rarely sees tearful, emotional scenes in the Gospels. Jesus simply tells people to follow Him, and I think He says the same to us. Your desire to give your life to Christ is largely a rational one. You listened to what I had to say, you believe what you have heard to be the truth, and you want to respond on that basis."

"So the lack of emotion doesn't matter?"

"Not at all. Some people, it is true, are led to God through an emotional experience. Yet a rational, intellectual yielding to Christ is in some ways even more powerful than an emotional one since the will itself plays a more determinative role. C.S. Lewis, one of the great Christian spokesmen of the last century, came to Christ, as he describes it, completely on the basis of logic and without a speck of emotion."

"All right, then...I am ready to proceed."

The pastor's office fell silent for some seconds.

"God," began Taggart in a surprisingly unaffected tone, "I want to thank You for Rev. Jefferson's openness in explaining to me how You work. And now, as he has told me about it, I want to repent of my sins. Even though I've lived a good enough life, I realize that by ignoring You I have been living in sin just as much as if my sin had been more flagrant. So I would like to ask You to forgive me. I know that You do because that is why Your Son Jesus died on the cross. And—"

He paused, then glanced up.

"I'm sorry, Rev. Jefferson," he said, "I'm afraid I drew a blank. What else was there?"

"Just tell Him what you are thinking," answered Jefferson, "and then invite the Spirit of Christ into your heart."

"Oh yes...right."

Again Taggart bowed his head and closed his eyes.

"And, Jesus," he said, "I thank You for dying for me. And now I want to ask Your Spirit to come into my life and live with me. I receive You as my Savior. Help me to begin living with You in charge of my life. Thank You."

Again he looked up.

"Did I cover everything?" he asked.

"You did very well," smiled Jefferson. "Congratulations. Welcome to God's family."

———◆———

Brock Yates telephoned Yvonne a little after eleven on Saturday morning.

"I need to go see Jill today," he said. "Would you like to come with me?"

"Jill...why Jill? What's it about?" asked Yvonne. She was still a little irritated that Brock had gone someplace with that Tolek geek after last night's game.

"I'll explain when we get there."

"All right...I guess so," she reluctantly agreed.

When the three were together an hour later, Brock immediately explained to Jill the reason he was there.

"Something happened to me," he said. "I had an encounter with some-one that...well, it jolted me, I guess. It showed me that even when you're young like us and have all your life ahead of you...that you never know, that unexpected things can happen...you just never know what the future's going to hold."

The girls listened silently, not sure what Brock was getting at.

"I guess I'm not making much sense," he went on. "Okay, it's this—I realize that maybe I need God in my life."

He paused. Yvonne was staring at him with huge eyes of disbelief. Her Brock...the hunkiest guy in the school...talking about God!

"Maybe it's that I *want* God in my life," Brock added. "I can't say why, but I think it's right."

He paused briefly, then looked at Jill.

"But...do you remember," he continued, "what the minister said last Sunday, about being born again? He said there was no formula, so I don't exactly know what to do next."

Jill nodded. She remembered what Pastor Jefferson had said.

"The interesting thing is that when Nicodemus asked how to be born again, Jesus gave him no formula. He compared being born again to the wind.

"That analogy says to me that this process of inviting the Spirit of Jesus Christ into one's heart and beginning to live as God's child, is an invisible process that each man and woman must discover for him and herself."

"I guess that's where you come in, Jill," said Brock. "You've been going to church a long time. You're the only person I know to ask. So...what do I do?"

"I don't know...what do you mean?" said Jill, a little embarrassed at Brock's bluntness. She couldn't help wondering what Yvonne was thinking.

"Well...I mean, it's a little confusing," said Brock. "He talks about God and Jesus and the Father. I can't keep them all straight. Who exactly is God, anyway...and who is Jesus? Who is it that comes into your life?"

"I'd never really thought much about it," replied Jill.

"What do they teach you in church?"

"Well, that Jesus is God's Son, I guess."

"So...does that mean that the Father He talks about is the same as God?"

"I don't know," she answered. "That's always confused me a little too. There's a thing called the trinity that kind of explains it."

"What's that?"

"It means that God is sort of three persons at once, or has three different personalities or something—the Father, the Son and the Holy Spirit. God is all of them, but they do different things."

"This is more complicated than I thought," said Brock. "So...who is the Lord?"

"I think that can refer to either Jesus or God...or God, the Father, I mean," said Jill.

"Why do they call Him that?"

"It's a title or something, I guess."

"And who are you supposed to pray to?"

"I don't know—I think you can pray to all three, or just to God. I've heard people pray to them all."

"And so who do you ask into your heart?"

"Jesus, I think...well, Jesus' Spirit."

"So is that the same as the Holy Spirit?"

"I don't know...I guess."

"And then when he talks about obedience, who are you supposed to obey?"

"Jesus, I think...well, and God too, because Jesus said He obeyed the Father."

It was silent a moment. Brock shook his head. "Well, I guess I can figure all that out after I learn more. Right now I suppose I just ought to get on with it. I don't suppose you'd ever get anywhere if you waited until you understood every detail. When I was a freshman, the football playbook was more complicated than this. But that didn't stop me from starting to play, and now I know it by heart.—So, Jill," said Brock, glancing up and looking straight into her eyes, "will you pray with me?"

Jill sat as one stunned.

"Uh...*pray* with you?"

"Yeah. I want to be a Christian. Tell me what to do."

"I don't know...I hardly know how to pray myself."

"You know more about it than I do. I'm ready to give my life to God."

Jill could not help thinking of her own prayer of just yesterday. Yvonne continued to listen in irritated silence, though the interview was striking deeper root within her than Yvonne herself realized.

"Uh, all right, then," said Jill, drawing in a deep breath. "Um...I guess just pray and ask Him to come into your life."

"Ask who?"

"Jesus...or God, I guess."

"You mean, just say it?"

Jill nodded.

"With my eyes closed?"

"I don't think it matters."

"Okay," said Brock. "Then here goes…"

Brock closed his eyes.

"Uh…well, God," he said, "I'd like to ask You to come into my life. And You too, Jesus…both of You, I guess. I want to be a Christian.—What else?" he said, glancing up at Jill.

"About your sins," she said.

"Oh, yeah.—And forgive me for my sins, and help me to do better from now on…"

"And open your heart to Him," added Jill.

"That's right," said Brock. "I remember him talking about the door of your heart."

Again he closed his eyes.

"I open the door of my heart to You, God," he said, "and ask You to come in and live inside me."

He paused and the room of Jill's house was silent a long while. Yvonne was more embarrassed than she had ever been in her life.

"And I pray for…well, You know who," said Brock at length, "that You'll take care of the situation with him and that You'd keep him from…well, just maybe that he'd see that he needs You too. Amen."

Brock opened his eyes and looked up. Jill smiled.

"Okay, well…thanks, Jill," said Brock, standing up. "I've got to be going." He headed for the door. "I've got to go see someone. You want me to take you home, Yvonne, or you want to stay here at Jill's?"

"Who are you going to see?" she asked.

"That guy…Trent Tolek."

"What in the…is he like your best friend all of a sudden?" said Yvonne sarcastically, then left the house, letting the door close behind her a little more loudly than usual. Brock watched her go, then looked back at Jill with a shrug.

"Thanks again," he said.

Jill smiled. She felt warm inside, and was really happy.

"I guess we ought to pray for Yvonne, huh?" Brock added.

"Yeah," nodded Jill, "I think we should."

Sally Parker had been back to The Answer Place several times. She had talked to the lady there, Mrs. Carter. But she hadn't quite got up the courage to divulge her problem.

They'd talked a little more personally last time, and when she was leaving Mrs. Carter had given her a sheet with a list of verses on it. Sally had read it several times since. It was mostly about salvation.

That was all fine, Sally thought. Salvation, maybe...but what then? She had more immediate problems than just her soul and whether she was going to go to heaven or hell.

Was God for people like her?

Frankly, eternal life just wasn't that big of a deal to her. Maybe when she was older it would matter more. But now...she had enough trouble just making it from one day to the next. Who cared about heaven when life itself was hell? Could God ever make her feel good about herself again? Would she ever know healing, and what it was to feel clean?

Sally glanced at the top of the sheet again.

"God," she prayed, "I do want to know Your truth. I ask You to reveal Yourself to me. If I can't find help from You, where else can I turn? I know I am hungry, but I'm still not sure You can help me. What Mr. Jefferson calls the abundant life...how can I ever experience such a thing? How can it be for people like *me*?"

Quietly Sally Parker began to cry. She hadn't cried for years. She had learned long ago to squelch every emotion that tried to rise within her. Yet even the strange warm flow of tears brought with it no feeling of warmth like Jill Chin had felt. If God was anywhere, He did not seem to be in the room with her right now. Her prayers might as well have bounced off the ceiling and fallen back down on her head.

Never had she felt so isolated, so alone, with nowhere to turn for help.

Faintly into her memory came a few of the words of Lynne Jefferson's poem...

How can I know this truth you speak of?
Where do I meet this God you call love?

If she only knew the answer to that question, thought Sally. Where was it one met God?

More words from the poem gradually filtered back into Sally's brain.

He's not far to seek if you'll but make a start.
In fact, you'll discover Him in your very own heart.

But He *didn't* live in her heart, thought Sally. She wasn't a Christian. She was nothing!

That's where He will dwell if you'll open the door.

Was that the key? thought Sally. Could it be as simple as one little word...if?

...if you'll but make a start...if you'll open the door.

Making a start...opening the door. Was it all a choice? Was it up to her? Was it something she had to *decide* to do?

"I never had a choice!" she said angrily to herself. "I was too young when it started."

Then quietly came the thought..."You have a choice now."

Sally turned and again picked up the sheet of verses Mrs. Carter had given her and scanned down it. Wasn't there a verse like that...something about opening a door?

There it was...Revelation 3:20. Sally read it through again. "I stand at the door and knock. If anyone hears My voice and opens the door, I will come in..."

Was God knocking on the door of her heart? she wondered. Was that why she felt this way? Was that what had been going on these last two weeks—God knocking at her heart?

Did she—Sally Parker, victim of incest, lonely and depressed—did she matter so much to God that He would actually care enough to speak to her personally?

The idea was too much to take in.

Did she actually *matter* to someone?

That God might really love her...care about her...so much that He would speak to her, trying to tell her He cared about her...how could it be!

Again tears came to Sally's eyes. This time they did not stop.

"All right, God," she said quietly, "I'll take You at Your word. There is still so much I don't understand. I don't know how You can love someone like me, or what You can do with me. But I want to open the door of my heart and invite You in. So I do. Please come into my life and live with me."

She paused and was silent for several minutes, breathing deeply, trying to take in this thing she had done. At last she began to pray again, tears flowing in a steady stream.

"Oh, God," she said, "I need so much help! My life is all mixed up inside. Please, heal me and make me clean again—"

At the word *clean*, she broke into great sobs.

"...make me clean on the inside!" she wept. "Thank You, God, for loving me...thank You for being a Father to me whom I know will always be good."

———◆◇◇◆———

A certain passage of Scripture had been on Anne Jefferson's mind all day.

The words were tormenting her. She had come upon it in her regular Bible reading this morning. Ever since the memorial service and funeral, she had just been going through the motions in a daze of sorrow and grief. Her mind had hardly been capable of thinking of the man who had done this terrible thing. Maybe in time she would think about him...but not yet.

Despite her husband's request from the pulpit, she couldn't deal with that just now. She could not summon what it took to pray for the man.

But then, this morning the words leapt off the page from Matthew 5: *"But I tell you: Love your enemies and pray for those who persecute you."*

Words so familiar. Anne had known them since childhood. Now suddenly those ten words seemed to represent the very Mount Everest of human impossibility.

"Lord," she cried, breaking down in tears. "I can't do it...I just *can't!*" Anne broke down and wept.

"Lord...help me," she whispered through her tears. "I want to obey...but I just can't. This is so hard! I don't know if I can. You can't really mean it...to forgive someone who has killed your only child!"

Suddenly the words she had spoken sent a chill through Anne Jefferson's body.

Her tears dried, her eyes opened wide. She sat still and erect as if stunned suddenly awake out of a deep sleep.

She shuddered momentarily as the words from her own mouth echoed back upon her.

...has killed your only child.

Then followed the words of the familiar verse, suddenly alive with new and intensely personal meaning.

"For God so loved the world that He gave His one and only Son, that whoever believes in Him shall not perish but have eternal life."

"Oh God, oh God," cried Anne. "I am so sorry. You lost Your only Child too! The whole world put Him to death—"

Anne stopped again.

All at once the most bitter truth of all dawned on the minister's wife. As it did, she began to sob again with great tears of remorse.

"Oh, God, forgive me! We *all* put Him to death, the whole world...even *me*. I helped crucify Your dear Son too!"

She could hardly go on. "Forgive me," she wept. "And You do, don't You Lord? You forgave the whole world...and You forgave *me*. God, I am so sorry!"

For several minutes she wept as she had not wept even after Lynne's death. Gradually as she began to breathe more evenly, Anne Jefferson knew what she must do. If God's own example meant anything, if her daughter's life meant anything, she could not now turn her back on what might be the man's eternal destiny.

"God," she whispered quietly, "I will do what You say. But I cannot do it without Your help. Please, Lord...go before me...and give me courage to obey."

Hank Dolan sat on his bunk in his small isolated cell.

He glanced across at the one piece of furniture in the room other than the bed and toilet: a small built-in table. On it sat a paperback book. It had been brought to him two days ago by the girl's father.

The guy had wanted to talk. But Dolan hadn't been in the mood. He didn't want to get chummy with some teary-eyed wimp trying to get him saved. If the man had been a better father, he would have kept the girl from meddling in other people's lives.

He had not opened it, not even touched it, in those forty-eight hours. Yet just lying there, the book was driving him crazy. He could not stop thinking about it, looking at it...all the while tormented by the last words he had heard from the girl's mouth, *Dear Jesus...*

This was insane, thought Dolan. What kind of an idiot was he to let a ridiculous Bible twist and torment his mind, a foreign presence in the room like an eye looking at him. He was going to put an end to this once and for all!

He rose from the bed and walked to the table. He paused briefly, then reached out and picked up the book. A momentary tingle surged through his fingers.

Enraged, he spun around, exploding with a foul string of profanity, and threw the book with all his might against the far wall of his cell. It fell with a dull thud on the floor. The echo of his yells died out, and once again Hank Dolan was left in solitary silence.

And still the book lay there, silently accusing him of the sin he knew all too well lay in his heart.

Twenty-three

SATURDAY, NOVEMBER 1

6:43 P.M.

Lane Rakestraw realized that even with his church background, there had never really been a single moment in his life when he had made a public profession of his belief. So many parts of the sermon kept coming back to him.

"Another myth that has come down to us through the years is that salvation comes instantly in a single moment of conversion. But if you read through the ministry and teachings of Jesus, you gain a beautiful picture of what is often a gradual and steadily deepening maturity of life with God. It was certainly gradual in the lives of the disciples. The teachings of Jesus always emphasize the growing lifestyle rather than the instantaneous experience."

Was he one of those whose salvation had continually deepened through the years?

Lane Rakestraw knew he wasn't.

So why not begin that growth now? The longer he put it off, the slower the process would be.

Lane bowed his head and began to pray.

"Lord," he said, "I believe in You, and I think I always have. Help me to now take that belief all the way down inside me to trust in You and have faith in You. Help me to begin *living* what I believe, not just believing it in my head. I don't really know whether I have ever actually invited You into my heart before. So just to be sure, I do so now. Jesus, please come into my heart and live with me. And I ask for Your help in growing as a Christian. I want to begin moving toward that deepening maturity he spoke of, so that today is the beginning of something that will last for the rest of my life. Thank You...amen."

———◦◦◦———

Scott Peyton was thinking about the sermon too. But it sounded too evangelical for him. He was not used to talking about God so personally or using the name *Jesus* so freely instead of something more formal like "the Lord Christ."

Was all this "personal relationship" business, and such an emphasis on being born again...for Catholics too? It wasn't how he'd been taught growing up going to mass.

And yet...he couldn't doubt that his conscience was making him wonder whether his years as a good Catholic were going to be enough to get him past Saint Peter standing at the gates.

———◦◦◦———

That same evening, Yvonne Seymour sat alone in her bedroom. This was the first Saturday night she hadn't gone out with Brock in ages. He was still somewhere with Trent Tolek.

Yvonne found herself thinking about Trent Tolek's sister. There was a geek if ever there was one.

But after listening to Jill and Brock talk to God, all at once Yvonne felt a stab of something she had never felt before. Her conscience stung her for calling the girl a geek, even if she had just done so to herself.

What right did she have to think that way, just because the girl wasn't pretty and popular? Then slowly began to rise within her something else she had never felt before—a wave of compassion.

Yvonne shook her head and tried to force the thought away. Feeling sorry reminded Yvonne of how mean she had been to people at the bottom of the "popularity food chain" at school. And feeling sorry for people wasn't pleasant.

But she couldn't make the thoughts go away. She felt bad for how she had treated Lidia.

Now her face rose in Yvonne's mind's eye, a sad, lonely face. She could almost imagine Lidia with tears in her eyes. Yvonne recalled incident after incident when she had ignored her, brushed by her without so much as a look, or made some deriding comment to Brock as they passed her in the hall.

Then the minister's words returned to her.

"Salvation may, of course, begin in a single moment. For those who have never done so, the Lord can be invited into one's heart in a brief prayer that takes but a few seconds. Let me remind you, too, that many who have been attending church for years may never have actually prayed such a prayer."

Slowly tears began to come into Yvonne Seymour's eyes—tears of remorse for her self-centered attitude.

The poor girl, thought Yvonne. Lidia Tolek couldn't help what she looked like. How would she feel it *she* were fat and homely instead of thin and pretty?

Was that why Brock was spending time with her brother? Had he begun to see that maybe popularity wasn't everything it was cracked up to be, that maybe people mattered more for who they were on the inside than the outside?

The next words out of her mouth shocked even her. For all at once, alone in her room, Yvonne Seymour quietly began to pray.

"God, I don't even know if I like this," she said. "At first I thought Brock was crazy to be thinking about You so much all of a sudden. But maybe I was wrong. I don't even know what to pray. I can't say for sure that I know whether You're real or not...but I guess if You are I want to know it. So please, show me if You are there. And if You are, please come into my heart and make me a better person. And I want to repent of my attitude toward poor Lidia, and I pray for her too. Amen."

Tracey Keane walked slowly toward her car. Her shift at the market had ended ten minutes ago.

All day she had been thinking about tomorrow morning and whether she ought to go to church again. But she knew she'd already decided. Of course she would go. She wanted to hear more about what Rev. Jefferson had to say about being a Christian.

But there was something she needed to do first.

He had explained about asking God to be part of one's life.

"A prayer of acceptance of Christ in your own words might go something like this.

"I thank You, God, that You love me, and I thank You, Jesus, that You died for me. I acknowledge my need for You and my belief in You. I ask You to forgive my sins. I thank You for forgiving me. I receive You and accept You, Jesus, as my Savior and Lord, and invite Your Holy Spirit into my heart to dwell with me there. I relinquish the right to self-rule in my life. I ask You to help me. Draw me closer to You and help me to grow into the man or woman You want me to be. Help me, Father, to be Your child, to obey You and to do what You tell me."

Tracey knew as she sat listening that she wanted to do it. But something had prevented her. Maybe she just hadn't felt quite ready yet.

But now she realized she was. She was tired of being lonely. She wanted to share her life with God. And as she walked along the sidewalk, she knew there was no reason to delay longer.

"God," she said to herself as she went, "I want to share my life with You. I ask You to come in and be part of it. I know I need You. I have been alone for so long. I accept You and ask You to come into my heart. Help me to grow closer to You and to be the kind of person You want me to be. Forgive me for my sins, even ones I am unaware of. Amen."

Tom Kingston also was thinking about church tomorrow…and about last week's sermon. God had his number, and Tom knew it. He'd dug himself in pretty deep. But he'd heard enough sermons in his life to know that there was no hole so deep that God couldn't get you out. And he knew it was high time he reached up, took God's hand and tried to start climbing up out of the pit he was in.

Harlowe Jefferson's words from last week were still fresh in his memory.

"Learning to live in relationship with God takes the rest of a lifetime. There are, though, three important ways one cultivates this new life.

"Praying and talking to God is the first.

"Reading the New Testament to discover the kind of life Jesus wants His followers to live is the next.

"And finally, obeying what God tells you to do.

"Pray, read your Bible, obey—do these and you will grow as a Christian."

Tom realized that up till now his Christianity had been a mere intellectual exercise. No wonder he had landed in so much trouble. He had never really *lived* his faith. He hadn't made prayer a priority. He didn't read Christian books. He had never gone through the Gospels to find out what he was actually supposed to *do*. The Bible his parents had given him at his high school graduation still looked new. He had done none of these things. No wonder he hadn't grown.

He believed the Christian message. But he had never placed his trust in it or done *anything* about it. He had just let it stay inside his brain as head knowledge. And when push came to shove, ethical and moral slippage had been the result of his spiritual laziness.

"God," he said, "I've made a mess of my life. I've hurt a lot of people in the process, my family most of all. I'm sorry. Forgive me. I want to turn it around. I want to start over. It's time I laid down self-rule in my life and started letting You call the shots. Help me, Lord, to do what You tell me. Right here and now I yield my right to independence. I turn over the throne of my life to You."

Tom let out a long sigh.

"And I pray, Lord, for Barbara and the girls," he said. "Barbara's got every right to leave me. But, God, I pray that somehow she would be able to forgive me too."

He paused and his thoughts continued to dwell on his wife.

He would tell Barbara...he would tell her tonight, tell her everything. Painful though it would be, if he was going to make a start, he had to start with the truth. And maybe next week he should go to his accountant and lay it on the line. If bankruptcy was on the horizon, they had better start making plans for it.

Earlier that afternoon, Carole Laudine had ventured into the store called The Answer Place, not without a little fear and trepidation. Her image of a Bible bookstore prior to that moment was vaguely like that of a front for some kooky cult group.

She walked through the doors, surprised to hear peppy music playing and a bright upbeat atmosphere surrounding her. She found her way first to the cards and before long had picked out two or three she really liked.

"Hello," said a friendly voice behind her.

She turned to see a woman approaching with a smile.

"Oh, hi," she replied.

"Let me know if there is anything I can help you find."

"Oh, uh, thanks...I've never been in before...I just wanted to look around."

"Sure...let me know if you have any questions."

As she reflected back on the incident that evening, the history professor was reminded of Rev. Jefferson's words of the previous Sunday just before the end of his sermon.

"And speaking of growing as a Christian, if you don't already know it, make acquaintance with The Answer Place. Read good books. They will help you enormously. Don't order them by mail, go into the store. Christian fellowship takes place everywhere Christians gather. I know of no place other than church where you will benefit so much from being with other believers as in a lively Christian bookstore where the Spirit of God is vigorously at work."

She smiled as she remembered glancing at her watch during last Sunday's service as the pastor began to conclude his message, surprised to see that it was only quarter till twelve. Not that she'd heard very many sermons in her life, but this certainly had to be one of the shortest on record.

Would she go back tomorrow morning?

She would have to think about it. Right now she wanted to get started in this book she had picked up at the store this afternoon. Its title had struck her immediately, *Does Christianity Make Sense?* The subtitle read: "Answers to Questions About Christianity by a Skeptic."

She sat down in her favorite chair and began to read from the author's introduction: "If you have purchased this book, you no doubt have serious reservations about Christianity. Like you, I was once a skeptic. I thought the

Christian faith couldn't hold up logically and rationally. I fancied myself an intellectual who had progressed beyond the constraints of some outmoded religious system that was irrelevant in our modern times. Once I looked into it, however, I began to see how wrong were my impressions. For in fact Christianity is the only world religion capable of withstanding the most rigorous scrutiny of rational intellectualism. I soon discovered it to be a thinking man's religion if ever there was one..."

When Rex Stone left his adult bookshop Saturday evening about eight, a little slip of paper fell to the ground. He stooped to pick it up. It had apparently been wedged between the doorknob and doorjamb sometime during the afternoon. Who had put it there?

He began to read. It was handwritten, apparently a poem.

The Bible is truth, for it is God's book...

What was it with this town, he said irritably to himself. The do-gooders were always interfering with everyone else's business, always trying to get everyone saved.

He tossed the paper to the ground where the wind picked it up, blowing as it listeth, and carried it across the street.

An hour or two later, Wolf Griswold left his motel room and began walking aimlessly toward the adult bookshop.

As he crossed the street, a piece of paper blew up in front of him. Just as it did, the wind died down and it came to rest at his feet. He stooped to pick it up.

He scanned it quickly, a few words coming off the page at him.

...the Bible is true, and God's love is for you!

Absently he crumpled it, stuffed it into his pocket and continued on his way.

188

The moment Tom walked into the kitchen, Barbara Kingston saw on his face that something serious was on his mind. The pain and hurt she felt at what she had learned suddenly gave way to fear. Was he about to tell her…that he was leaving?

Tom glanced about. When he did not see the girls, he went straight to Barbara and took her in his arms.

"I've…I've got a few things to tell you," he said. "I don't care if the dinner gets cold, I've got to get it over with."

His words certainly did nothing to alleviate Barbara's anxiety. Nervously she followed him into the living room. Whatever she was feeling herself, Tom seemed even more tied up in knots. He walked about the floor for a minute, drawing in several deep breaths, trying to muster the courage to begin.

"I don't exactly know where to start," he said at length. "The Lord has really been hammering away at me, and I…I have some things to tell you that aren't going to be pleasant…"

Twenty minutes later, both of them in tears, Barbara rose and walked across the living room. She opened her arms and stretched them around her fallen but repentant husband.

"I am so sorry!" said Tom, holding her tight as he wept. "I don't deserve your forgiveness…but I am more grateful than I can tell you."

"It's all right," said Barbara softly. "Of course it hurts. It will always hurt. But we will get through it…we'll get through it *together*."

"Thank you…I love you. I'm sorry I forgot how much."

"I love you too, Tom. I don't think either of us will forget again."

Twenty-four

SUNDAY, NOVEMBER 2

11:31 A.M.

Hearts were stirring all around town. More invisible mental wheels had been set in motion throughout Destiny Junction than even any of those faithful Christians who had long been praying for their community could imagine.

Why the crosscurrents of eternity had intersected at this place and this time, none of those who were being swept up in the drama could know. The *whys* of that world usually remain beyond the ken of human sight.

But for whatever reason, suddenly nearly everyone in the small town found themselves thinking in new ways about the unseen spiritual world. Most had no idea where these stirrings were leading. Only God knew that. But none could deny that the very air seemed filled with a magnetic energy turning eyes upward and waking consciences inward.

When Harlowe Jefferson took the pulpit on the Sunday morning a week following his sermon on salvation, this time he was more prepared for the sight that met his eyes.

"I see once again," he began, *"that we have many visitors and newcomers among us. Welcome to you all.*

"A week ago, following closely on my daughter's death," he continued, *"I felt compelled to speak on the subject of salvation. That I did so surprised even myself, for it was not what I had planned. But it seems to have been*

timely, for the church has had a steady stream of inquiries and calls all week, and many individuals have come to see me personally. As familiar as the term 'salvation' is, it seems there remains a great deal of uncertainty about just exactly what comprises salvation, how one enters into such an experience, as well as how one can be assured that he or she is in fact born again.

"What I would like to do this morning, therefore, is simply review in brief terms the various elements that I see comprising this thing the Bible calls salvation..."

As Rev. Jefferson went on, Dixie Judd thought about the words of the tract she had read. Could such a thing really be true, that God loved her as if she were the only person in all the world? For her and her alone, Jesus would still have died that *she*, Dixie Judd, might have eternal life?

She was ready to invite Him into her heart, thought Dixie. She would go talk to the pastor after the service.

Almost the same moment she remembered what he had said last week, about prayer being something you could do any time, at any place, alone or with others, eyes open, eyes closed. So why should she wait until the service was over? Why not pray right now?

"Dear Jesus," said Dixie silently, "I invite You into my life. Thank You for dying for *me*. Help me to live for You. Amen."

A strange feeling of contentment came over her. A faint smile came to her lips. God *did* love her. Somehow she could sense it.

"Are You...really inside me now, Lord?" she asked silently. "Was it really that simple?"

Yes, came the answer into her heart. *Yes, Dixie, you are My child now, and I am your Father.*

While Dixie Judd was praying, Annette Gonzales was thinking about what trust in God really meant.

Did *she* trust God? she wondered. Had she placed Sam's future in God's hands...or her own? Sam had told her what he had done outside the Christian bookstore. They had gone over the list of Scriptures from the sheet together, looked up every one in their family Bible, and then she had prayed to invite God into her life too. But she had still been struggling with Sam's cancer. How could God let such a thing happen?

"God, help me to trust You," she now prayed. "I turn over our future to You. If You really are a good Father, like they say, who loves us, then You will take care of us and make good come of it somehow. Be with Sam, Lord, and help him get better. But no matter what happens...help us to trust You."

As she sat in the congregation listening, Carole Laudine knew Rev. Jefferson was speaking to her. She also was thinking about the book she had bought yesterday. She was exactly the kind of person who had always considered herself self-sufficient and in need of no one else. She had been up half the night reading an account of the most fantastic intellectual journey to faith. It was like nothing she had ever encountered in her life.

She was scholar enough to know that truth alone was not the only factor involved. Truth did not exist in a vacuum. Real life was involved. *Response* to truth mattered most of all.

Even if Christianity was true, she realized she could continue to ignore it.

Or...she could act upon it. It was a matter of the *will*. The decision whether or not to respond was completely in her own hands.

Carole remembered the image she had seen on a painting in the bookstore yesterday, of Jesus knocking on a closed door with no doorknob. Suddenly she almost felt a presence beside her. She knew it was the presence of the Lord, patiently waiting, to see what would be *her* choice, knocking on the door of *her* heart, a door that He would never force, but that had to be opened from the inside.

And today, as she listened to Rev. Jefferson explain once again about entering into what he called the abundant life, she knew that at last she was prepared to embrace this amazing life she had so long ignored, this life called Christianity.

"God, if You are real," she said silently, "I am ready to listen. Forgive me for my pride, I am ready to believe in You and even be Your follower if that's what it implies. But I need more help to go all the way with it. I need to be sure. So I open my heart and mind to You. I open that door You are knocking on. I ask You to help me know beyond any doubt that You are real and that Christianity is true."

Meanwhile, Sean Schaeffer was not struggling with salvation, but with the age-old dilemma of God's goodness. He had been wrestling with it for two weeks, coming dangerously close to anger toward God. He realized that in some ways his faith itself was on the line. Could he say, *God is good*? If he could not pray a prayer of gratefulness, he would eventually become bitter at what had happened.

Finally, as he listened to Lynne's father, the struggle reached an internal climax.

"God," said Sean, tears rising in his eyes, "I thank You that You are sovereign and that You are loving. Give me a grateful heart. I affirm that You *are* a good Father, and that all You do will turn out for good in the end. Help me in my weakness, God, and light again the fire of my desire to serve You."

Bertie Snow, Jack Snow and Charlie Sweet had all come again to the service. The three skeptics sat in the back pew listening to the words coming out of the mouth of Harlowe Jefferson—three distinct wills poised to respond to his words and to the silent knocking on the doors of each of their hearts.

What would their choices be? Would they open those doors...or keep them locked from the inside?

What is each individual's eternal destiny? It was the question of the ages, which time and the circumstances of life must determine for every human who walks the earth.

Twenty minutes later, for a second consecutive Sunday after a sermon shorter than many anticipated, Rev. Jefferson began drawing his remarks to a close.

"*All these aspects of salvation we have discussed,*" he said, "*are involved in being born again. And many more that will be significant in certain lives. These are steps to a deeper life with God for presidents, grandmothers, children, laborers, teachers, secretaries, executives, financiers, homemakers and teenagers, not just for pastors and priests and those one usually thinks of as 'religious.'*

"*Salvation is for everyone. For you, my friends...and for me.*

"*Another thing about salvation,*" Jefferson added, "*is that it is ongoing. It is not a once-in-a-lifetime experience. Jesus may live in my heart, and I hope He lives in yours. But daily I must renew my commitment to yield to Him the throne of my life.*

"*I have to live out my salvation every day. There's no autopilot for the Christian life. Every day I have to engage my will to live as God's son and obey what He gives me to do.*

"*So you see, my friends...the invitation to God may be made in a moment. But the life of faith must be lived with fresh commitment daily.*"

Rev. Jefferson paused.

A long silence followed.

"*I will get personal a moment,*" said the minister at length, "*and tell you that walking with God is not always an easy life. Daily I must struggle to relinquish my own will. And what a struggle it has been these past two weeks for Anne and me to say to God, 'You are good...we trust You.'*"

As Sean listened, his heart stung him for his own struggle. How it paled in comparison with theirs! If this man and woman could keep saying *God is good*, then how could he not also affirm that resounding truth that held the universe together.

"God, You *are* good," said Sean silently. "You are a *good* Father."

"*Do you think that has been easy after losing our child?*" Rev. Jefferson continued.

"*No, my friends, it has been—*"

Unexpectedly the minister's voice caught, and he turned away. The congregation sat still and silent, those who knew him best in agony for the man they loved as they saw his shoulders begin to shake as he wept before them.

The next instant his wife was on her feet. Tears streaming down her face, Anne walked to the front of the church, took one of his hands and stood for several long moments beside him.

Gradually the storm of emotion passed. Anne handed him a handkerchief. Her husband dabbed at his eyes, then turned again toward the congregation. He drew in a quivering breath.

"*I'm sorry, dear friends,*" he said haltingly, wiping at his eyes again. "*Really, Anne and I are doing pretty well under the circumstances. We do believe that God is good. Yet there are times when suddenly the memory of what happened rushes in like a wave and overwhelms us.*"

Anne Jefferson continued to stand at her husband's side in front of the church, her hand resting in his.

"*What I wanted to say a moment ago,*" Jefferson went on, "*is that salvation is not always easy. This is no cotton candy faith, this thing called Christianity. Men and women have been tortured and died and suffered through the ages for no other reason than that they were known as Christians. Our Lord won no cheap salvation when He died for us on the cross. He prayed to be spared that cruel death. But in the end, because He trusted in God's infinite goodness, He said, 'Not My will, but Yours be done.'*

"*No...it is no cheap grace, but a hard-won salvation. I have been a Christian for thirty-five years. Some of you may think that my being a pastor somehow makes it easy for me, as if I've been given a discount card for life's hardships. But I am a weak human being like all the rest of you. It is no easier for me. Two weeks ago Anne and I lost our only daughter."*

He drew in a deep breath, blinking hard.

"Easy?" he said in a husky voice, and the tears flowed in earnest again.

"No...not easy. But it is right, because this gutsy thing we call Christianity is true. God is good. And we can trust Him. And you can trust your lives to Him."

A long pause followed.

"Trust Him, dear friends. Give Him your hearts. A moment ago I was going to say, 'Don't let Lynne's death be in vain.' But now I say, 'Don't let Jesus' death on the cross be in vain.' Invite Him to share life with you...and trust Him."

He wiped his eyes, then bowed his head.

"Dear Lord," he prayed, *"thank You for loving us in our weakness. Thank You for Your salvation in all its wonderful facets. Open our eyes to recognize our need for You. Help us to trust You, our Father. Amen."*

Still hand in hand, the Jeffersons began walking down the aisle together toward the door of the church. As they did, one by one a few in the congregation began to stand, then more, until the entire congregation was on its feet, not in praise, but rather as a silent ovation of honor toward this man and woman who had been through so much.

Twenty-five

10:25 A.M.

Bruce Penley had been on the job at Kingston Construction for three days.

Tom Kingston had been keeping a close eye on him. It was not his practice to hire itinerants. But this guy seemed different. Already he had learned enough of the ropes to be able to hold his own with the rest of the framing crew. It was obvious to everyone that he had worked in construction before.

At lunch hour the new hand sought out the boss.

"Say, Mr. Kingston, you mind if I talk to you for a minute?"

"No, Penley, what's on your mind?"

"It ain't about the work, other than to tell you again how grateful I am that you're giving me a chance like this."

"You swing a hammer as well as any of my men," laughed Tom. "I figure I'm getting my money's worth. But you got something other than work on your mind?"

"Yeah, I reckon I been thinking a lot about some of the stuff that Rev. Jefferson said. I was going to ask him about it, but then when I was sitting in his office, I guess I got a little, you know…embarrassed, him there with a fancy suit and tie, and me just a homeless man with only the shirt on my back. But then you seem like a down-to-earth fellow…I mean, you're a working man, and you ain't afraid to get your hands dirty. But according to the reverend you're a churchgoer and a religious fellow too—"

Tom's conscience smote him at the words. How could this man have any idea how deeply he had been struggling with his own lack of practical faith.

"—and so what I wanted to ask you," Penley continued, "was how a fellow like me gives his heart to God like he was saying. It sounds like something that would really help me, and I think I want to do it."

Tom could hardly believe what he was hearing. Was this man asking *him* how to accept the Lord?

"Believe me, Penley," Tom faltered, "I'm a worse sinner than you."

"That could hardly be if you been going to church all your life," rejoined Penley with honest sincerity.

"Church people are sinners too, Bruce. And I've been one of the worst—a hypocrite."

"Maybe so. But I still figure you can help me."

Tom was silent a long while, then remembered the previous Saturday evening and the prayer he had prayed.

"Well," he said at length, "maybe the Lord can help us both. So what is it you want to ask?"

"What does a fellow do?" asked Penley. "I want the kind of life Rev. Jefferson's talking about. Will you help me, Mr. Kingston?"

"I'll try, Bruce," replied Tom. "But I'm sure you could do better with someone else."

"Well, I figure the Lord must have put you and me together 'cause he saw fit for you to give me a job," said Penley, "so I guess I'll take my chances."

"All right, then, I'll pray with you and I'll pray for myself at the same time," said Tom. "And I think the first place to start in my own case is to ask for forgiveness."

"I reckon that'd work for me too," said Penley, " 'cause I ain't paid much attention to God all my life, and I done a lot of things I wish I hadn't."

"Jesus died for those sins of ours, Bruce. I'm sorry about many things too."

"So how do you ask forgiveness?" said Penley. "What do you do?"

"Just pray and tell God you're sorry, that you want to do better, and ask Him to forgive you."

"Well, then, I reckon I'd like to do that. Is there anything to stop us from praying right now?"

Tom glanced around and thought for a moment.

"Come into the trailer with me," he said.

He led his new worker inside and closed the door.

"I'm afraid there's only one chair," he began, looking around.

"The floor will do me just fine," said Penley. "I doubt if the Lord's sitting on a chair right now either."

Both men sat down. The small makeshift office fell silent for several minutes.

"Lord," Tom began at length, "we come to You together, just a couple of men who know they are sinners and know they need You, and we ask for Your help. You know I've never prayed like this with another man before, and I doubt Bruce has either. So we don't really know what we're doing, Lord. We just ask that You'll listen to our hearts more than our fumbling words, because both of us do want to do what's right."

He paused. Again it was quiet.

"That's right, God," now said Penley. "That's just how it is with me too, and I ain't never prayed before neither. I reckon I'm a little old, but I gotta start sometime, so I ask for Your help too, just like Mr. Kingston said. And I want to tell You how sorry I am that I waited so long, and I'm sorry too about the poor Jefferson girl. But I want to invite You to come to live with me now, in my heart, like the reverend talks about."

"And I too, Lord," said Tom, "want to give myself to You in a new way from this day on. I renew my commitment and rededicate my life to You."

"And forgive me for my sins too, God," added Penley. "I remember him talking about that. I repent of what I been and what I done. I repent 'cause I really am sorry, Lord, and I thank You for dying for those sins of mine."

"Amen," said Tom, nearly moved to tears. "I repent too, Lord Jesus. Forgive me."

A long silence followed.

"Anything else we ought to pray, Mr. Kingston?" asked Penley at length.

"I think the Lord knows our hearts, Bruce," said Tom, drawing in a deep breath and wiping his eyes. "Just keep talking to him like Rev. Jefferson said, and try to do what you think He wants. That's what I'm going to be trying to do myself."

A police squad car pulled up in front of Destiny Junction Community Church. A large man got out, then leaned back down through the open door.

"You want to come in, Charlie?"

"No," answered Sweet. "I'm just the delivery boy. You go on ahead, Jack."

The Deputy Chief walked to the church alone.

"Hello, Rev. Jefferson," he said when he saw the minister.

"Good afternoon, Mr. Snow. What brings you here?"

"I thought you ought to know that they're moving Dolan to the jail in Chambers on Friday."

"Thank you, Mr. Snow," said Rev. Jefferson. "I appreciate your letting us know."

The big policeman hesitated.

"Do you mind if I ask you something?" he said.

"Of course not," replied the minister.

"Is…you know…salvation, like you've been talking about these last couple of Sundays…is it for everyone…even a tough cop like me?"

"Yes it is, Mr. Snow—it is for everyone. Is there anything specific you'd like to ask?"

"Uh…not really, I guess. It's just that I never thought about it much…being born again, you know…a man like me who could take care of himself."

"None of us can take care of ourselves as well as we think we can, Mr. Snow," smiled Jefferson.

"Yeah, maybe you're right," said the policeman. "Yeah…well, I'll think about what you said."

As soon as he was gone, Harlowe Jefferson telephoned his wife with news of the development.

"I've got to try to see Dolan again," he said, "even if he said he doesn't want to talk to me."

"I think I'll go with you," said Anne.

As the two police officers drove away, Charlie Sweet noticed that the Deputy Chief was unusually quiet.

"What's up, Jack?" he asked.

"What do you mean?"

"You haven't said a word."

"Just thoughtful, I guess…"

He hesitated, then added, "I mean, haven't you been thinking about everything he's been talking about?"

"Who?"

"The minister…Rev. Jefferson."

"You mean about…salvation…all that born-again stuff?"

"Yeah."

"Naw," replied Sweet. "I figure there's plenty of time for me to think about it later. I don't need God now. I'm still young enough to take care of myself."

Twenty-six

A knock came to the door of the rectory behind Sacred Heart Catholic Church.

Father Kimble went to answer it.

"Mr. Peyton," he said, greeting his parishioner with a smile and a handshake. "This is a pleasant surprise."

"I wondered if I could talk to you, Father," said Peyton.

"Of course, Scott...come in and sit down."

As soon as they were seated, the insurance agent began.

"I don't know how closely you've been following events," Peyton said, "but I've been to three services at the Community Church in the last couple of weeks. At first I just wanted to show my respect for the Jeffersons. But I have to tell you, Father, some of what the minister says has really gotten to me."

"Rev. Jefferson is a good man," said Kimble.

"I wanted you to help me understand, from the perspective of a Catholic, all this about salvation and being born again. I mean, is it the same for Catholics?"

"Do you mean, do we need to be born again too?"

"I guess something like that."

"We certainly do," said the priest. "The salvation of Christ is for all men."

205

"What I mean, then, is...well, the personal relationship thing...you know, inviting Him into your heart," said Peyton. "That doesn't sound very Catholic. I've never heard you talk like that. I suppose that's the part that confuses me."

Father Kimble smiled.

"I may use slightly different terminology," he said, "but it amounts to the same thing. Yes, Catholics need to ask God's Spirit into their hearts too."

"I have never done so, Father, and I've been a Catholic all my life."

"You may be one of those with which the Catholic Church is filled. Actually, many Protestant churches are filled with them too."

"What is that?"

"Faithful churchmen and women who are not Christians."

"You mean...I might not be a Christian at all, even though I've gone to church, done the cathechism, been an altar boy."

"That's right. It is quite common."

"You mean...if I died right now, I might...you know, go to hell or purgatory instead of heaven?"

"I don't know about that, Mr. Peyton. I try to leave such things in God's hands. All I am saying is that being a Catholic doesn't make you a Christian any more than being a Methodist, a Unitarian, a Buddhist or a Rotarian. Being a member of a church is no different than being a member of a lodge or a country club or a political group if the Spirit of God isn't living in your heart."

"What makes you a Christian then?"

"A personal relationship with God and His Son Jesus, in which you have accepted Christ as your Savior."

"That sounds so fundamentalist," remarked Peyton. "Is that actually a Catholic doctrine?"

"It's not Catholic at all."

"What—you're confusing me, Father."

"It is a *truth*, Mr. Peyton—not a Catholic doctrine or a Protestant doctrine—but a truth that comes straight out of the Bible. That so few Catholics, or Protestants for that matter, realize the importance of it doesn't make it any less true for you and me."

"Well, as I said, I've been a Catholic all my life…but I want to be a real Christian."

"I'm sure you *believe*. You say so at every mass when you recite the creed. But believing and following are different. Jesus said follow."

"What should I do?"

"Why don't we pray together, Mr. Peyton, and you can become a Christian right now. Then you will be the best kind of Catholic of all—one who has Christ living in his heart."

Peyton thought a moment.

"What exactly is involved? What do I have to do?"

"Nothing more than open your heart to Him—if that is what you want to do."

"I…I think it is."

"Then why don't we pray together? I'll help you through it."

Father Kimble bowed his head and closed his eyes. Peyton did likewise.

"Holy Father in heaven," began the priest. "I thank You for Your child, Scott Peyton, who desires to live in closer fellowship with You. As Your Spirit has drawn him, I pray that You would continue to draw all Your children. And now be close to him as he takes this step as Your son.—Why don't you pray now, Mr. Peyton," he said, speaking to his visitor. "Dear God our Father—"

"Dear God our Father," said Peyton.

"I thank You for Your love for me, and for Your Son Jesus Christ who died for me…"

"Thank You for Your love," repeated Peyton, "and for Jesus Christ who died for me."

"We believe, as the creed says, in the Holy Spirit, the Lord, the giver of life. I want now to ask Your Holy Sprit into my heart..."

"I ask Your Holy Spirit into my heart."

"I take Jesus as my Savior and Lord..."

"I take Jesus as my Savior and Lord."

"And I ask You to help me obey Your word..."

"Help me to obey Your word."

"Amen."

"Amen."

Both men opened their eyes. Father Kimble smiled.

"That wasn't so difficult, was it?"

"No...not really," laughed Peyton. "Is that all there is to it?"

"That's all there is to inviting Christ into your heart," replied the priest. "But that step is only the beginning of living as one of His followers. You see, from this moment on, everything changes. Your life is no longer your own. You are God's man now. You are under new orders. You have to behave as God's men behave."

"But what about the church...now, I mean?" asked Peyton. "Are you saying it is unimportant in the life of a Christian...or a Catholic?"

"Not by any means. The church will now become even *more* significant in your life. Rather than a mere ritual or membership in a club, the church will become a means for you to grow closer to God in your daily life. The church was established to help Christ's followers obey Him more fully. That is its purpose. You will begin to hear in the mass, in the eucharist, in the Gospel readings, that His very personal message of love for you has been there all your life."

"So then...what should I do?"

"Read the Gospels, discover what Jesus told His followers to do, then obey. In your personal life, in your business, in your thoughts and attitudes, in your priorities and motives. It is really quite simple. The Christian life is not about going to mass or being a good Catholic any more than it is about being a good Protestant or evangelical. It is only about one thing—doing what Jesus said."

"Well, Father, you have given me much to think about," said Peyton as he rose to leave. "Thank you."

As the priest watched him go, happy as he was to help a man come to Christ, Father Kimble thought how unfortunate it was that salvation was not something they taught you much about when entering the priesthood. He wondered how many of his faithful parishiners were in the same boat.

In his tiny motel room, Wolf Griswold sat with suitcase open on the bed as he assembled the parts of his Remington. Only another couple of days. He'd gotten the word that they were moving Dolan. He had to be ready.

Beside the suitcase was a crumpled piece of paper he'd found in the street.

When he was satisfied, he stuffed the rifle under the bed and went out for a last walk-through. He had located a spot overlooking the courthouse and jail building, the rooftop of an elementary school, easily accessible and with a foolproof getaway route. He already had a pair of janitor's overalls stashed there. After the hit all he had to do was mosey down and hang out in the school corridors, pretending to push a broom for an hour or so.

He'd be so obvious right under the cops' noses, they'd never suspect him.

Later that same day on Cedar Street, several passersby observed a sight that a few of them considered incongruous: a Catholic priest walking through the doors of the Destiny Junction Community Church. He immediately sought the pastor's study, and the two old friends greeted one another with an affectionate embrace.

"What brings you to my humble office, Lawford, my friend?" said Jefferson, offering Father Kimble a seat.

"One of your sermons," replied the priest. "The ripples of your salvation message have widened to encompass those in my church as well, and have brought some confusion along with them."

"Oh no," rejoined Jefferson. "Have I misspoken? I hope I have not offended—"

"Set your mind at ease, Harlowe," said Father Kimble with a gesture of his hand. "The confusion raised is entirely a healthy one. I must say, I wish I could have heard your two sermons," he added. "The whole town, it seems, is talking about them."

Jefferson laughed lightly. "Isn't it amazing," he said, "that the subject of being born again, which many would consider boring, has suddenly aroused so much interest?"

"As I said, the people in my church are talking about it too. As familiar as the topic is, there is still a great deal of confusion."

"So many who consider themselves to be Christians," nodded Jefferson, "deep down are very unsure about their own standing with God."

"That is especially true among Catholics," rejoined Kimble. "We don't teach much about conversion. But that is why I came over. I had a visit from one of my parishioners about an hour ago, your own insurance agent, Mr. Scott. I thought it would bless you to know that, because of your salvation message, he has just given his heart in a new way to our Lord."

Kimble went on briefly to recount the gist of his conversation with Scott Peyton.

Jefferson smiled. "Thank you for sharing it," he said. "One never knows what people are thinking and how they are responding to what you say. Of course I don't need to tell you that."

"The misconception of people," said Father Kimble, "about being faithful churchgoers versus being disciples of Jesus Christ is truly the most difficult aspect of the priesthood for me."

"It's the same way everywhere," said Jefferson. "How many Methodists or Baptists or Episcopalians do you think have actually prayed a prayer of salvation? The problem is widespread even in an evangelical church like mine. The churches of the world are filled every week with millions who never have."

"I fear Catholics and evangelicals alike play at religion without realizing they are doing so," said Kimble. "I say that with no malice. For the most part they are good, sincere, upright people, dedicated and loyal to the church. I would even say they are dedicated and loyal to the cause of Christ. They simply haven't been taught about what being a Christian really means."

"Do you suppose that might be because they are dedicated to the cause of Christ but not to Christ Himself?"

"A good insight," nodded Kimble. "My people are so hung up on the notion of being what is called *a good Catholic*. I have come to loathe that phrase."

"No less than mine about being a good *evangelical*," rejoined Jefferson.

"In a way, it's not even their fault," the priest went on. "But even so, it still prevents them from progressing in the Christian life. Spirituality cannot penetrate all the way into their hearts because the Holy Spirit has never been given access to that innermost region in order to carry out His life-changing work. If only they had prepared us for this dichotomy when we prepared for the priesthood."

"I never learned this in seminary either," said Jefferson. "Even the most evangelically correct institutions major on ethics and doctrine and methodologies and religion in modern culture and sermon preparation and Greek and Hebrew and Church history and comparative religions...but rarely salvation."

Father Kimble laughed. "I am encouraged to hear that you struggle with the same thing. Sometimes I think I am alone.—But I need to be going, my friend. I just wanted to stop by briefly." Father Kimble rose, then looked deeply into Jefferson's eyes.

"How are you holding up, Harlowe?"

"The Lord is getting us through it. You know the saying, One day at a time."

"And Anne?"

"She is struggling. The pain is deep, Lawford, as you can imagine. But every day we wake up and find ourselves a bit more accustomed to the change. To put it in its simplest terms, you gradually *get used to* it. Even tragedy is something the human mechanism accustoms itself to as time moves forward. God has placed remarkable adaptability into the human species. After enough days, somehow you begin to breathe again."

"You are in my prayers."

"Thank you. That means a great deal."

"Give Anne my love."

"I will, Lawford. Thank you so much for the visit."

————◦◦◦————

It had been an extraordinarily beautiful afternoon, a true Indian summer's day.

The moment Sally Parker got off work, she changed clothes, grabbed her camera bag and went back outside. A day like this had to yield some spectacular photos...if she could just find them. And the sunset should be wondrous!

She checked her small plot of roses. Only a few blooms were left by now, and none attracted her interest. She would try the field next door. A thistle in full flower, perhaps...an intricate spider web...who could tell.

Margaret Sanderson saw her neighbor and realized she was out for a photo walk.

The other woman picked up her cane, then went downstairs, outside, and into the grassy meadow behind the apartment complex.

Sally saw her approach, lowered her camera and smiled.

"Hello," said Margaret. "Taking pictures?"

"It's my hobby," replied Sally. "I make greeting cards with them."

"I've seen you out a number of times. I live right over there."

"Oh, then we're neighbors. That's my house," said Sally, pointing behind her. "I'm Sally Parker."

"I'm happy to meet you, Sally," replied Margaret with a smile. "My name is Margaret Sanderson.—My husband used to be quite a photographer too."

"What kind of pictures did he take?" asked Sally.

"Nature photographs, black and white mostly."

"Do you still have them?"

"Oh, yes—I have his entire collection. Would you like to see them?"

"Very much," replied Sally enthusiastically.

"Would you like to come over to my apartment for a cup of tea?"

"You mean...right now?"

Margaret nodded.

"Are you sure it wouldn't be an imposition?"

"Of course not. I would love the company."

"All right, then. I would like to see your husband's pictures. Is he—"

"No—he's been gone for some time now."

"Oh...I'm sorry."

Margaret turned and they began walking back toward the apartments together.

"Didn't I see you at the Community Church last Sunday?" asked Margaret as they went.

"Yes, I was there."

"I thought so."

"Actually, though, I'm not a member," said Sally. "I was just visiting."

"So was I. I hadn't been to church in years before that."

"What prompted you to go?"

"A lot of things. Lynne Jefferson's death mostly, I suppose."

"Really—that's how it was for me too."

The two women chatted freely as they continued on, then climbed the stairs to Margaret Sanderson's apartment.

Twenty-seven

WEDNESDAY, NOVEMBER 5

4:37 A.M.

Hank Dolan awoke. It was the middle of the night. But he did not know what time it was. Day…night…everything was the same here. A thin yellow light invaded his consciousness. Slowly he opened his eyes.

He was sweating and agitated. Whatever had caused it, he only knew that it was very quiet, and that he felt alone.

What had disturbed his sleep?

It must have been a nightmare. All his brain could call up were vague images…words…silent words…colored words…flashing over and over… some kind of message…soundless and unbidden.

Now he knew them. They came from red neon signs that blared their garish slogan above a hundred skid rows in a hundred nameless cities where he had bummed what he could before moving on, in a few places getting into such bad trouble with the mob that he had to run for his life…signs erected above a hundred run-down, inner-city rescue missions plugging their worn-out spiritual wares.

Jesus saves!

The gospel reduced to two words in flashing red neon.

These were the words that had disturbed his sleep with their silent assault against his self-made exile from mainstream society.

Over and over the words now flashed in his brain...*Jesus saves...Jesus saves.*

The message was unwelcome...intruding even here. Could he not escape it even in jail!

Jesus saves!

Now more words...words from childhood...biting deeper...probing...accusing...inviting....pounding with increasing force against the barriers of his arrogant self-sufficiency.

He clasped his hands to his ears, trying to block them out. But still they rang inside his head. Words which, by their very import to one who might soon be on death row, could not be ignored.

For God so loved the world...His one and only Son...whoever believes...not perish but have eternal life.

Hank Dolan shook his head, trying to clear it. He had to wake out of this nightmare of tormenting words ringing like a noiseless celestial alarm clock that had gone off in his cell.

Eternal life...eternal life...

He jumped to his feet and walked around the small enclosure like a caged tiger, trying to escape that from which there was no escape.

Suddenly a voice spoke his name...*Hank Dolan.*

In terror, Hank spun around, thinking the guard was at the door.

But no one was there. He was alone...fearfully alone.

Hank Dolan, came the voice again.

Again Hank spun about. He had never been afraid of man or beast in his life. But he was afraid now. Frantically he turned in every direction, scanning his cell for sign of some presence.

"Where are you?" he cried with eyes wide in fright. "*Who* are you?!"

I am the Lord. Why are you persecuting Me?

"I...I don't—" Hank began to say aloud.

His own voice suddenly jolted him like a splash of icy water. The sound woke him as from a trance. For an instant normalcy returned. He saw the cell empty and quiet. He stood in the middle of it breathing hard.

He drew in a long breath of relief, then let it out slowly. Whatever was going on, it seemed to have passed. This was insane, he said to himself. No one was here. Who had he thought he was talking to?

He was going crazy! His brain was playing tricks on him. He had imagined the whole thing.

But suddenly the Voice spoke again. It hardly mattered whether the sound was audible or came from some unknown place inside him. Hank Dolan heard it just the same.

Hank, it said. *I am the Lord. I love you...I want to give you life.*

He nearly leapt out of his skin, spinning around wildly.

"What have You ever done for me!" cried Dolan in a passion of terror. "Go away. I want nothing to do with You."

Again the words shot into his mind as if fired from some distant memory-gun out of his past. *For God so loved the world...so loved the world...*

"I don't want Your love," Dolan yelled, his voice now one of panic and fury and terror all in one. "You may love the world, but what is that to me? No one loves a killer. Not even You! My father hated me. Everyone hates me. Show me one person in the world who loves me...then I'll listen! Go away...go away!"

Suddenly silence descended once more. Hank Dolan was aware that the cell had become empty. The Voice was gone. He was alone again.

Relieved, though still sweating and breathing heavily, he returned to his bed, lay down and soon fell again into a fitful doze.

Twenty-eight

WEDNESDAY, NOVEMBER 5

9:00 A.M.

Four hours later, Anne and Harlowe Jefferson approached the city jail. Anne looked up at the building and drew in a deep breath to calm her last-minute hesitations. Despite the church's jail ministry, she had never actually been inside. She could not help being apprehensive.

Deputy Chief Jack Snow was on duty. He greeted the pastor and his wife as they entered.

"We would like to see Mr. Dolan," said Jefferson.

Snow nodded, then led them upstairs.

"Do you mind, Harlowe?" said Anne as they went. "I would like to see Mr. Dolan alone for a few minutes. It is something I think I am supposed to do."

Her husband glanced over at Snow, as if to ask if he thought it was safe.

"I'll be standing right outside the cell door," he said. "She'll be fine."

<hr />

"Dolan...Dolan..." came a voice into Hank Dolan's sleepy brain.

In terror, Hank tried to clear his brain. But he was still half asleep. Had the Voice come back to torment him?

"Dolan...you got a visitor."

Now the sound was familiar...close and more real than before.

The prisoner came a little more awake, then turned groggily over on his bed. There stood the big form of Jack Snow over him. A lady was beside him. Still confused, he blinked a time or two, wondering if Snow had been responsible for the earlier incident.

"Dolan, get up," said Snow. "This is Mrs. Jefferson...she wants to talk to you."

The policeman turned and left. Dolan sat up on his bed. The name had not registered. Anne stood awkwardly.

"Mr. Dolan," she began, her voice shaky, "I wanted to see you...I would like to give you a New Testament. I hope you will read it."

She held out a small book. He did not know it was the same one Lynne had offered him before.

But the nightmare and rude awakening had made Hank Dolan surly. The words *New Testament* grated on his brain like fingernails on a chalkboard. It reminded him of the Voice.

"Forget it, lady," he said irritably. "What do you want from me?"

"I want nothing, Mr. Dolan," she began, tears rising in her eyes. "I only—"

"Come on, lady...if you're gonna cry, go somewhere else and do it. I don't need it."

"I'm sorry, I only..."

The minister's wife was full of too many conflicting emotions to speak. Still Dolan was unmoved.

"What's this all about?" he groused. "Who are you anyway? What are you doing here?"

Finally Anne Jefferson found her voice in the midst of her tears.

"I...I am Lynne Jefferson's mother," she replied softly.

The words jarred Dolan where he sat. The visit from the girl's father had done nothing to soften him. But now suddenly the mother's tears went straight to his heart. Why the sudden change, who could say. But all at once something inside the heart of the hardened criminal opened a crack. As it did, a shaft of light pierced through at lightning speed and seared his soul.

Inwardly Dolan began to tremble. He felt a return of the peculiar sensations that had nearly driven him out of his mind in the middle of the night.

"If you won't take this Testament," said Anne, continuing to speak with a trembling voice, "I don't suppose I can make you. But I want you to know...as hard as it is to say it...that by God's grace, I...I forgive you, Mr. Dolan."

The words struck Dolan's ears like thunderclaps. In the momentary silence of the cell, he felt as if the universe of the only world he had ever known was crashing down on top of his head.

Unconsciously, his hands grabbed at his face and covered it. What was that warmth he felt in his eyes? Had he heard what he thought he had heard? She...*forgive* him!

I forgive you...forgive you...forgive you.

Then more words came into his spinning brain...words from his dream. *For God so loved the world that He gave His one and only Son...*

Then followed the memory of words from his own mouth. *Show me one person in the world who loves me...then I'll listen.*

Hank Dolan's brain spun out of control. His face was hot. He could feel his body shaking. He was losing control of himself.

Suddenly in the midst of his turmoil, Dolan felt a touch. It sent a surge of warmth through his body. He lowered his hands and looked up. It was the woman's hand on his shoulder. Her cheeks were wet with the tears of obedience.

"God loves you, Mr. Dolan," she said softly. "He gave His only Son to die for your sins so that He could forgive you and so that you could know eternal life with Him."

The words of love that had so infuriated him from the daughter such a short time earlier, out of the mouth of the mother, now at last found their mark. The eyes that sought hers were red and moist and full of disbelief, confusion and wonder. Only a second or two more, then Hank Dolan broke down weeping where he sat.

Anne waited for several seconds.

"Would you like to know His forgiveness, Mr. Dolan?" she said gently.

Helplessly, like a child who has lost his way and is willing to take the hand offering to lead him home, he nodded. Head again cradled in his hands, he continued to cry.

"Then why don't we pray together right now?"

He nodded.

"Dear Lord," said Anne, "all we can know at a time like this is that You see our hearts. You know them better that we know ourselves. You know our every weakness, our every sin, mine as well as Mr. Dolan's...and yet You love us and are eager to forgive us. More than that, You are eager to shower Your love upon us...if we will only come to You. And now, dear Jesus, I ask that You would give Mr. Dolan the strength many men do not have—the courage to unburden himself to You and come to You humbly and with repentant heart, laying his sins at the foot of the cross where You died for him, so that You may take him to Your Father to be made clean and whole."

She paused.

"Are you ready to pray with me, Mr. Dolan?"

"I...think so," he said softly, his voice quivering. He no longer sounded like a murderer but a little child.

"Then ask Him to forgive your sins."

The cell was quiet for a few seconds. The next words from Hank Dolan's mouth were the very words for which he had shot Lynne Jefferson. And yet now her prayer was answered out of his own mouth. He spoke them with the tender humility of the second thief on the cross.

"*Dear Jesus,*" he said in a shaky voice he could still not quite control, "I'm sorrier than I can say for what I've been...for the life I've lived. I been about as bad as a man can be. I don't know...how You could forgive a sinner like me...but if You can...I ask You to."

He began to cry again, deep wrenching sobs coming from some long buried place within him.

"Tell Him that you accept Him as your Savior because of His death on the cross for you," said Anne.

Dolan wept a few more seconds before he could find his voice.

"God, I'm so sorry," he said, still sobbing, "for what I done! If this lady can forgive me...then maybe You *can* forgive me. So I accept Jesus as my Savior...because He died for me on the cross."

"Then invite His Spirit into your heart."

"And I invite His Spirit to come into my heart."

"Then thank Him, Mr. Dolan, for giving you eternal life."

"Thank You, God...I know I don't deserve it...I ain't sure I can believe it, but I thank You...for giving me eternal life."

Anne stepped back and stood patiently for a few moments. Dolan continued to tremble and weep quietly, then gradually calmed. Finally he looked up.

"I don't know what to say, Mrs. Jefferson," he said sniffling, eyes red. "No one's ever cared for me all my life. I don't know how you could do what you just done."

"That's the kind of God we have, Mr. Dolan. He gives us strength to do the impossible."

"I can't tell you..."

He looked quickly away, bitter tears stinging his eyes. Now more than ever, he could not look into the face of the woman whose daughter's life he had taken.

"...how...how sorry I am!" he said. He began to sob again.

"Without God's grace, I could never have forgiven you," said Anne, again placing a tender hand on his shoulder. "But because God forgives, we too can forgive. And because you have now accepted His love, Mr. Dolan, your sins, as well as mine, are washed white as snow."

That same night, alone in his bed staring up at the ceiling, Deputy Police Chief Jack Snow relived the extraordinary encounter he had overheard in the jail that morning. He had been standing outside Dolan's cell and had listened to every word. He had been thinking about it all day. It was the kind of encounter that could not help but change even a tough cop like him.

What that lady had done was the most remarkable thing he had ever witnessed in his life. His own eyes had filled with tears at the sound of Hank Dolan crying like a baby, and the minister's wife telling him she forgave him.

He remembered Charlie Sweet's words—*There's plenty of time for me to think about all that later. I don't need God now...*

How different was Dolan's response.

Charlie Sweet had been to church now three times, just like him. He had heard the same message as Hank Dolan. Yet Charlie said it wasn't for him.

Snow thought about himself. Which would be *his* response: To heed the invitation...or wait and think about it later?

The policeman lay a long time in silent reflection.

How could you ever know what the future held? Life was too uncertain. If you were going to do something, if you *knew* you wanted to do something...why wait until later?

Especially something as important as salvation and one's eternal destiny.

What did *he* want? thought Jack. Did Jack Snow want salvation...or, like Charlie Sweet, did he figure he didn't need God yet?

It didn't take him much longer to decide. As much as he liked Charlie, he was going to follow Hank Dolan's example, not Charlie's.

"God," said Jack Snow quietly as he lay in the darkness, "I thank You that Jesus died for me. I know I need You and I ask You to forgive my sins. I thank You for loving me. I accept Jesus as my Savior. I invite You, God, into my heart. I'll do my best to try to live for You from now on. Make me the man You want me to be, and help me to do what You tell me."

Twenty-nine

FRIDAY, NOVEMBER 7

8:42 A.M.

Two days passed. The town of Destiny Junction awoke on Friday and began to go about its business. Its streets gradually filled with school buses and traffic, people on their way to work, students walking and biking to their morning classes at the college.

Wolf Griswold's bags were packed. He was ready to split. He had been in this place long enough for five jobs. The sooner it was done and he was gone, the better.

Charlie Sweet went on duty at 7:00.

Wolf Griswold walked into the motel office at 7:19 to check out.

After patrolling the streets for an hour, Officer Sweet headed back to the station for his most important assignment of the day—transporting Hank Dolan to the correctional facility in Chambers.

His uncle had informed Bertie Snow of the transfer. The young journalist arrived with notepad about 8:15.

Whatever he found to write about would hardly be a scoop. The Jefferson shooting was the most sensational news to hit Destiny Junction in a long time. The transfer would offer the public its first opportunity actually to see Hank Dolan. Leslie Cahill and a camera crew headed by Lane Rakestraw drove up in a Channel 3 van at 8:20 in preparation of capturing the event for that evening's news.

Harlowe and Anne Jefferson also had been notified. They had their own reasons for wanting to be on hand. They arrived at 8:30.

A sizeable crowd began to gather.

Their friend and family physician, Dr. Sarah Woo, was standing with the Jeffersons at 8:42 when Deputy Chief Snow brought Dolan, in handcuffs, downstairs and outside. The television cameras rolled as they slowly made their way out of the jail. Sweet approached, took hold of Dolan's arm, and, with the two policemen flanking him, the prisoner walked to the waiting car.

Suddenly, from out of nowhere, two shots exploded in the morning air.

Screams and shouts erupted through the crowd of onlookers. The few officers who had been standing guard drew their guns yelling and glancing frantically about. Almost immediately the building behind them emptied of police officers.

The screaming crowd scattered in every direction.

Rakestraw panned the area with his camera, trying to capture the sudden pandemonium.

"Where'd it come from?" shouted Snow as he glanced about.

"Anybody see the shooter?" cried another.

"Check the roofs!"

Already several squad cars were squealing off, sirens blaring.

In the seconds following the shots, it had not registered in Jack Snow's brain just how close to death he himself had come. But now suddenly he realized that beside him, Dolan had collapsed.

Snow glanced down. The prisoner lay motionless on his back. Red blood was splattered all over his chest.

"Get an ambulance!" shouted Snow over his shoulder. "Dolan's been hit."

Suddenly he saw that on the other side of Dolan also lay a blue police uniform on the ground. He jumped over Dolan's form and knelt down.

"Oh, Charlie...Charlie!" said Snow. "Charlie, can you hear me?"

Sweet's eyes were open but glazed over. It was obvious he was in a bad way. A faint trickle of blood oozed out of his mouth. A gaping wound revealed that his stomach had been blown wide open.

"Oh God...Charlie...hang on, buddy! Help's on the way."

Dr. Woo ran toward the scene to see what she might be able to do. She flashed ID to the swarm of police officers. While Snow was attending Sweet, she knelt beside Dolan. The cluster of blue uniforms quickly closed about them, every eye on their fallen comrade.

She examined Dolan's wound but saw instantly that he needed more help than she could give. He needed surgery, and fast.

Woo glanced into his face. He was still alive, and he seemed to be trying to speak. She bent closer.

"The lady..." croaked Dolan in a barely audible voice, "please...get the lady..."

"What lady?" said the doctor. "I can barely hear you."

"Please...the lady...minister's wife..."

"Mrs. Jefferson?"

Dolan closed his eyes and nodded imperceptibly.

Dr. Woo jumped to her feet. Pushing through the blue uniforms, she ran to where the Jeffersons still stood in shock.

"Anne," she cried as she ran up, "Anne...he wants you. Come quickly!"

Oblivious to the mayhem around them, and only knowing that his friend was dying, Jack Snow leaned close to Charlie Sweet's face.

"I...I thought...would be more time," whispered the patrolman, barely able to get out the words. "Jack...I didn't think I needed—"

He choked. Snow found his hand and gave it a squeeze.

"Hang on, Charlie...just hang on. We're gonna get you—"

"No time, Jack," he murmured with one remaining gasp of life, "too late...thought I'd have...thought God...thought there would be more—"

Suddenly his hand seized Snow's big palm with the final grip of the struggle.

"Oh, God—" cried out from Sweet's lips. Then sounded a long slow sigh as his lungs emptied.

Snow felt the vise of the man's fingers slowly relax. He looked into his friend's eyes and knew Charlie Sweet was gone.

Jack Snow broke into tears. Several of the officers peering down at the scene turned away, wiping their eyes.

Beside Snow, though he was hardly aware of it, Sarah Woo tried to stop the bleeding in Dolan's chest while Anne Jefferson knelt and bent low. Dolan labored to speak.

"Wanted to say...your daughter...didn't mean...so sorry...thank you for...forgiving...at peace...story of two thieves..."

Weeping, Anne took his hand and nodded.

"He loves you, Mr. Dolan...He will take care of you."

"...the one he said...about paradise...I think—"

Dolan's words ended abruptly in a wince of pain followed by silence. One look at his face and she knew he was dead.

Anne wept. Behind her, Harlowe Jefferson slowly drew her to her feet. She nearly collapsed in his arms as they left the scene.

"What did he mean?" asked Dr. Woo, who rose and walked away with them.

"He gave his heart to the Lord the day before yesterday," said Anne, as she continued to cry. "I think he was trying to tell me that he had made his peace with God like the thief on the cross."

Dr. Woo took in the words soberly. If such a man like Hank Dolan can open his heart to God, she thought, how can I be so proud as to think I don't need Him?

Meanwhile, Jack Snow still knelt beside the body of the man who said he would think about God later.

"God, take care of poor Charlie," he whispered. "I don't know what You do with people who put off salvation till it's too late. But—"

The scream of an ambulance siren roared up, interrupting his prayers. Snow stood and turned toward the sound. It was was too late for the paramedics to do much good here now.

That afternoon a nondescript sedan drove along the interstate fifty miles north of Destiny Junction at a comfortable fifty-seven miles per hour. Nothing about the car or driver would call attention to itself as being anything out of the ordinary.

On the passenger seat sat an empty pizza container, a soda can and a rumpled piece of paper with a handwritten poem that for the past couple of days had curiously drawn the attention of the man behind the wheel.

He glanced over at it again, then rolled down his window, took the cardboard pizza holder and tossed it outside. The can followed onto the side of the road. Finally with his right hand he grabbed the paper, crumpled it into a tight wad and sent it out the window with the rest.

Thirty

Saturday, November 8

11:01 P.M.

The town of Destiny Junction was still abuzz on Saturday about the shooting outside the jail.

Everyone except for Trent Tolek. He had heard about it, of course, and that the assassin was still on the loose. But none of it concerned him.

He had his own destiny to face...and he knew this was the day.

It was now or never.

News of yesterday's events had jolted him with the realization that it still lay within his power to carry out, if not the first half of his plan, at least the last phase...the part concerning himself.

He remained alone in his room most of the day with the door closed.

The rifle he had so carefully assembled was lying at the bottom of the river, thanks to Brock Yates.

But he still had his pistol. No one knew about it, thought Trent as he turned the .32 revolver over in his hand, then slowly inserted a bullet into the first chamber. He turned the cylinder and inserted a second, then a third, until all six chambers were full.

He would need only one, he thought as he pensively turned the loaded weapon over in his hand. But he still liked the idea of being ready for anything.

Slowly the day passed. A deeper sense of melancholy than usual gradually came over him.

As the afternoon progressed, a rising restlessness came over him. He was anxious to get it over with.

Evening came. Night fell. Then darkness.

His sister had been watching him all day. She was worried. Trent had always been strange. But today seemed different.

About 9:30, Trent heard something under the door of his room. He glanced over. Someone had slipped a sheet of paper beneath it. He went and picked it up. It was a handwritten note from his sister.

Dear Trent,

I read this verse in the Bible today. I thought it might mean something to you. It goes: *For God so loved the world that He gave His one and only Son, that whoever believes in Him shall not perish but have eternal life.*
Lidia.

He shrugged, then crumpled it up and threw it in his trash can.

About eleven, Trent snuck quietly from his room, tiptoed down the stairs and left the house. In her room, Lidia was listening. She could not help being scared. She got out of bed, dressed and followed him.

Trent walked out of the housing development toward the river, then out onto the bridge. Even now he still hadn't decided how to do it, whether to use the gun or jump off the bridge. Probably the gun. He couldn't be sure about the river.

He reached the middle, then stopped.

For a long time he stood gazing out. There was no moon, and not much light from the distant streetlights. He couldn't see the water, but he heard it faintly below him. How long he stood he didn't know...ten minutes...twenty. He lost track of time. He was not exactly thinking, just waiting. Not for anything...just waiting.

Slowly his hand crept into his pocket. His fingers touched the gun, then wrapped around it. Slowly he pulled it out.

His heart began to pound. Feeling the cold steel reminded him of the finality of what he was about to do.

Why now...but all at once he remembered Lidia's note. Its words came into his brain. *For God so loved the world...loved the world...loved the world...*

He took in a deep breath, then raised the pistol and pointed the barrel against his right temple.

...loved the world...loved the world...

When did anyone ever love him? Trent thought...somebody love him? The sound of the word almost made him shudder.

Love.

Did such a thing really even exist?

Slowly his index finger felt the pressure of steel against it.

The face of Brock Yates now came into his mind...then his sister's. Maybe a few people cared, he thought. But would they even really miss him when he was gone?

...loved the world...loved the world...

Trent's hand began to quiver.

Come on, man! he said to himself. *Pull the trigger and end it!*

But another part of him had begun to do battle with the part of him that wanted to end it all. For several long seconds the battle waged. His sweating hand quivered, his finger poised against the lever that would bring about his own death.

Suddenly he pulled his hand back and with a great heave threw the gun from him. At the same instant a great cry echoed out in the night.

"God, I don't want to be alone anymore!" he shouted.

As his voice died away, a faint splash sounded below in the blackness. At the sound, Trent Tolek collapsed on the sidewalk. "Please, God..." he said, breaking down and crying like a child, "I don't want to die...please, help me...please come into my life...and help me."

He sat another fifteen or twenty minutes. Finally the tears subsided. He drew in several quivering breaths, then stood.

Slowly he began to walk back the way he had come. He was emotionally spent. What had just happened to him? Trent didn't know. His brain was fried. He couldn't think. His body trembled from the ordeal.

He saw someone in the distance, standing on the bridge. He continued on.

It was his sister. What was she doing here?

When she saw him, Lidia ran forward.

"Oh, Trent," she began, "I was—"

She broke into tears, then embraced him. Strangely warmed, Trent returned her hug.

"I was worried, Trent," she said after a moment. "I'm sorry...please don't be mad at me for following you."

"That's all right," he replied. "Forget it...it's okay."

They began to walk together off the bridge. It was quiet for a minute or two.

"I don't think I've ever told you before," said Lidia, "but I want to say it now—I love you."

"Why...what's got into you?" said Trent.

"Nothing. I just thought I ought to tell you."

"Well, okay," he said, "thanks. That's a nice thing to say."

"Shall we go home?" said Lidia, trying to smile.

"Yeah, I'm getting cold."

"Me too. You feel like a cup of hot chocolate when we get back?"

Thirty-one

MONDAY, NOVEMBER 10

8:49 A.M.

Bertie Snow sat staring at his computer.

Three days had passed since dramatic events had rocked the town of Destiny Junction for the second time in four weeks.

This was an even bigger story than the first he had written…if, as he had been struggling to do since the beginning, he could find the *real* story… the story behind the story.

But wherever he turned, from his Uncle Jack to the Jeffersons, what he was told had little to do with the shootings themselves…but with salvation.

He had tried from the beginning to separate the events from the spiritual side of this thing. But everywhere he looked, that was all anyone was talking about. Even his normally down-to-earth Uncle Jack.

And now a story had surfaced about Hank Dolan finding salvation.

Maybe he'd been wrong, thought Bertie. Maybe the *why* of this story was salvation after all.

He'd go to that bookstore again. Maybe he ought to do a little more research on this thing that had the whole town talking.

He'd ask the lady there to recommend a book that explained it in a little more detail. He probably also ought to pick up a Bible while he was at it.

There was no doubt that the big cop had been deeply affected by the death of his comrade, thought Leslie Cahill. But whether she would put the interview with Jack Snow on the air, she still wasn't sure.

Would the religious angle play one more time? That was all Deputy Chief Snow wanted to talk about—the remarkable exchange between the murderer and the mother of the young lady he had killed.

But maybe that was the story, thought Cahill. If so, she knew she would have to get it straight from Lynne's mother herself. Perhaps the minister's wife would even go on camera and tell what had happened in her own words. With the current climate of interest about town, an interview with Anne Jefferson would be a blockbuster.

She would go visit the Jeffersons today and try to get to the bottom of Hank Dolan's reported conversion once and for all. It would give her the chance to return Rev. Jefferson's Bible. It was time she bought one of her own.

Perhaps at the same time she could get straight in her own mind whether what she thought she heard in Rev. Jefferson's sermon was actually true—that she needed God just as much as a sinner like Hank Dolan. She was still a little confused about that. It didn't seem to make much sense.

But no doubt the Jeffersons could clarify it for her.

Dr. Sarah Woo had looked death in the face many times. It went with her job. But never, she thought, had she witnessed anything so moving as the poignant exchange between Anne Jefferson and Hank Dolan as he lay dying on the concrete outside the jail.

All she had been able to think since then was that if a man like Hank Dolan could open his heart to God, how could *she* be so proud as to think she didn't need Him at all?

Perhaps God was indeed answering the brief prayer she had prayed that Sunday morning in church. But was she ready to do what He was showing her?

She glanced at her watch. It was almost nine. Her first appointment of the day was probably already waiting.

Sarah Woo slowly closed her eyes where she sat at the desk in her office.

"God," she whispered, "I am finally ready to say *yes* to You. I realize I have been hiding behind my own respectability, using it as a crutch to keep me from looking beyond myself. I am at last ready to lay it down and admit that I need You after all."

She paused briefly and drew in a breath.

"Lord," she said, "I invite You to share life with me. I am making the decision as of this moment to be Your follower. I believe in You. I believe in Jesus…and I am ready to call myself a Christian."

Thirty-two

SUNDAY, DECEMBER 14

12:07 P.M.

The sights and sounds of Christmas were in evidence everywhere as the people of Destiny Junction Community Church made their way out of the sanctuary following the morning worship service. They had just sung "Silent Night." The congregation was slowly filing out of the sanctuary. Harlowe and Anne Jefferson stood at the door greeting those who exited.

Brock Yates and Trent Tolek had been sitting together. Brock had just come outside and was now waiting for Trent, who was visiting briefly with Rev. Jefferson behind him.

"I am so glad to have you and Lidia in our new disciples class," the pastor was saying. "I can tell you are a thinking young man. I have appreciated some of your questions and comments."

"It's all still new to me," rejoined Trent. "I'm just trying to make sense of it."

"I applaud you for that," answered Rev. Jefferson. "Too many Christians take what they are told without thinking it through for themselves. So having someone like you ask good hard questions is a breath of fresh air. You've added a great deal to the group."

"Thank you."

"Are you and Lidia coming to the youth group Christmas party this Friday?"

"I'll let you ask Lidia for herself," said Trent with a smile. "She's right back there. But I'll be there."

"Good...right...I see your sister with Jill and Yvonne—I'll ask them all. The Lord bless you, Trent."

"Thank you, Rev. Jefferson."

To the side, Sally Parker and Margaret Sanderson, who had come to church together every Sunday since their meeting in the meadow, were talking with the minister's wife.

"Jeanne tells me she plans to put some of your cards in her store," Anne was saying.

"I'm trying to get a dozen ready for a little display," replied Sally.

"And you, Margaret," Anne went on, shaking Margaret's hand, "how are you this morning? You'll be at the women's Bible study on Tuesday?"

"I wouldn't miss it," replied Margaret.

"Will you need a ride?"

"Thank you, but I'll be coming with Sally and Mrs. Carter."

"Oh, Sally, you'll be joining us?" said Mrs. Jefferson, turning toward Sally again.

"I don't have to be at work until noon that day."

"Wonderful. I'll see you both then!"

As Trent joined Brock outside, he found him talking to Richard Ray, whom they had met a month before at youth group but hadn't seen in a couple of weeks.

"Richard, where have you been?" said Trent as he walked up.

"I went back to see my folks," replied Ray. "I've been there a couple of weeks. I may move back home, but I haven't decided yet."

"You going back for Christmas?" asked Brock.

"Yeah," answered Richard. "I haven't been as good to my mom and dad the past few years as I should have been. So it's time I started making up for it."

"I know what you mean," nodded Trent. "Me too."

Behind them, Harlowe Jefferson was now shaking hands with the Gonzales family.

"How's the chemo going, Sam?" he asked.

"Not much fun," he answered, "but they think it's helping."

"How are you doing otherwise?"

"We feel better prepared for whatever the future brings, more at peace I suppose, than ever before," replied Sam. "Wouldn't you say, honey?"

He glanced toward his wife. Annette smiled and nodded.

"I think it may be harder for me," she said. "Sam is handling it great. I have to fight discouragement every day. But I remember what you always say, that God is good whatever circumstances look like and that we can trust Him."

"Well, we are all continuing to pray for you."

They filed outside, while the pastor continued to shake the hands of those behind them.

"Good morning, Tom, Barbara...and Mr. Penley—hello," he added to the well-groomed, clean-shaven man at Tom Kingston's side whom he hadn't recognized at first. "You're looking very well."

"I got you and Tom here to thank for everything," replied Bruce Penley. "And your daughter, too...and of course the Lord."

"Bruce has agreed to join my crew full-time," said Tom. "If he keeps it up, he'll be foreman of the framing team within a year."

"What are your plans for Christmas, Mr. Penley?"

"I'm going home to see my mother. I haven't seen her in way too long. I may even bring her back with me. She's alone now. I'm trying to find a place where I can take care of her and keep her with me."

"For now you're still living in the little apartment in back of Tom and Barbara's house?"

Penley nodded.

"Well, I shall certainly look forward to meeting your mother. Merry Christmas, Mr. Penley."

Meanwhile, Sean Schaeffer was making his way out of the church with three guests whom he now introduced to the minister.

"Rev. Jefferson," he said, "I would like you to meet my professor from seminary, Dr. Matthew Fellowes."

"Dr. Fellowes, I am pleased to meet you at last," said Harlowe Jefferson. "I've heard a great deal about you from Sean."

"And I you," rejoined Matthew.

The two men shook hands warmly.

"This is my wife Judith...and our daughter, whom I believe you know, Heather."

"Ah yes...hello again, Heather."

"Hello, Rev. Jefferson," smiled Heather, taking his offered hand.

"Anne...Anne, dear," the minister called out to his right. "When you can pull yourself away, there are some people here I would like you to meet."

Within a minute or two, the two wives were talking together like old friends.

"What are your plans for the afternoon?" asked Anne.

"Nothing in particular," replied Judith. "We'll be driving back to Chambers."

"Could you stay long enough to have dinner with us?"

"I don't see why not. I'll talk to Matthew."

Around the front of the church small clusters of people were visiting enthusiastically. No one seemed anxious for the fellowship to end.

Jeanne Carter was talking informally with banker Doug Taggart about the advisability of expanding the gift lines of her store to take in the small space next to it, which she had heard might be going vacant.

Tracey Keane and Dixie Judd, who had met at a singles group, were leaving together. They had recently discovered a mutual interest in miniatures and planned to spend the day creating a new pattern they were hopeful of being able to sell.

The unlikely group of Sarah Woo and Carole Laudine, with Jack Snow and his wife, were discussing Harlowe Jefferson's sermon. All four laughed in turn, saying that the last thing they had expected to be doing this holiday season was going to church and talking about the deep meaning of Christmas in their personal lives.

Toward the end of the line filing out of the sanctuary, a man no one in the church recognized, dressed in a plain black suit, approached the minister. Harlowe Jefferson extended his hand and smiled.

"Good morning," he said. "I don't believe you and I have met."

"My name's Stone," said the visitor. "Rex Stone."

"Well, Mr. Stone, we are very happy to have you with us this morning."

Meanwhile across town, Bertie Snow and Scott Peyton left the rectory of Sacred Heart Catholic Church together where they had gone to ask Father Kemble about starting a group for professionl men to study the Gospels from a down-to-earth and practical perspective. Both men shared with the priest their hunger to find out what Jesus really had to say…for them… today.

That evening, the youth group at Destiny Junction Community Church was lively and exuberant.

Lidia Tolek and Jill Chin, with Trent Tolek and Brock Yates, sang "My Sheep Were Grazing on a Plain" in four parts, to Richard Ray's accompaniment on the guitar. They had worked on the harmonies half the afternoon.

Yvonne Seymour, Lidia and Richard put on a Christmas skit—all three dressed up as wise men, trying to keep straight faces through the Halloween beards on their faces—though it was interrupted so many times by their own laughter that it took twice as long to get through as planned.

After a devotional talk by Anne Jefferson and a brief time of prayer, the meeting broke up in time for the evening service. Jill, Trent, Brock, Yvonne and Lidia made plans to eat lunch together the next day, then talked Richard into coming to the school to join them.

Carole Laudine submitted a proposal to Northwestern State College for a course to be offered the following term on the spread of Christianity in the ancient Roman Empire.

The doors of Rex Stone's shop did not open again following the Sunday of his appearance at Destiny Junction Community Church. He attended services regularly, became a member and was baptized six months later.

Richard Ray moved back home, resumed the music studies he had abandoned and enrolled in college the following year. He declared a major in music, and he hoped eventually to teach guitar and piano in the elementary grades.

Bruce Penley became foreman of the framing crew of Kingston Construction and made a down payment on a small house for himself and his mother.

Jill Chin and Lidia Tolek became best friends. Lidia never did get asked to the homecoming dance, but in her senior year was voted president of the Bible Club, a far more enduring honor.

Sally Parker's photographic cards were so well received in The Answer Place that Jeanne Carter began showing them to some of the visiting sales reps from several large card companies. Margaret Sanderson began writing the verses for the interior of the cards.

Heather Fellowes remained at home living with her parents and enrolled in the university at Chambers. After graduation she planned to go into some form of missionary work.

Annette and Sam Gonzales grew strong through their trial, though neither the chemotherapy nor radiation treatment was successful in entirely eliminating Sam's cancer. His future continued to be uncertain.

Tracey Keane and Dixie Judd quit their jobs at the market and the café. The space next to The Answer Place did in fact become vacant. The two opened a small gift shop together, and, with the overflow from Jeanne's business, it thrived.

Barbara and Tom Kingston entered a season of great financial struggle. They scaled back their business, took only small jobs Tom knew he could handle, and eventually managed to pay off most of their creditors. Barbara discontinued most of her church activities in order to take over the secretarial and bookkeeping duties of the company. Slowly they reestablished the business on a sound footing.

Trent Tolek graduated from high school, getting all As and Bs his senior year. He enrolled at Northwestern to study engineering, hoping one day to become an architectural contractor.

For God did not send His Son into the world to condemn the world, but to save the world through Him.

—John 3:17

The character of Lynne Jefferson is a composite of two friends of Judy's and mine, both taken from this world at a young age but whose lives continued to exercise an impact long after they had gone home to be with the Lord:

Lynne Martucci and Karen Jackson

To their memories we affectionately dedicate this book.

AFTERWORD

The town of Destiny Junction is not particularly unique. It is your town. It is my town.

Like all towns, cities, suburbs and communities, behind its doors and storefronts and stained glass windows, in its homes, its businesses, its banks, its malls, its schools, its grocery stores, its offices and its churches, live and work men, women and young people—all of whom thirst for the same thing, though most do not realize it. To the watching world they present a facade of self-sufficiency. But one never knows what personal stirrings may be at work beneath the surface of those one passes each day and what private dramas are being invisibly lived out before one's very eyes.

The vignettes and characters in this book are mostly based on actual people. The stories are not *factual*, and of course the names have been changed. Some of the incidents are real, many are fictional, and some are a blend between the two.

However, I believe in the reality of fiction. Books such as this may not be factual but nonetheless can often be *true*. Characters of a story can teach us about ourselves just as powerfully as people we meet every day.

So I say to *you*, dear reader, "God loves you and cares about you. You matter to Him. He can work in all lives and in all circumstances. If He can touch the lives of these individuals you have just read about, He can and will also touch yours. God is your Father. And the day will come, whether now or in the future, when the still small voice of that divine Fatherhood will make itself heard in your life as it did in hearts throughout Destiny Junction. At first you may not recognize the gentle knocking at the door of your heart and mind. But it will be Him, and He will be anxious to speak with you further if you will but turn your inner ear in His direction."

There are no formulas for walking in fellowship with God. Life with our heavenly Father is wonderfully personal. He draws every man, woman and child in a unique and individual way. Your life with God, and mine, will be unlike anyone else's, because God has a plan and a purpose just for *you* and *me*.

There are *many* aspects to salvation—including others besides those mentioned in this book. I have not tried to represent these as the only means by which one comes to God. Talk to the Lord about all that salvation means...and most importantly what He wants it to mean in your life. Seek good Christian books whose authors will broaden your understanding. Speak with men and women who have been on the road of faith longer than you, including, perhaps, the individual who gave you this book. Ask God to lead you. Seek guidance daily from the Gospels, from the mouth of Jesus Himself. If you ask for His help and are willing to do as He tells you, He will speak to your mind and heart. His Voice may be tiny and quiet at first, until you learn to recognize it and respond to its gentle urgings, but He will speak. Then, in proportion to your obedience, will His voice become louder and more discernible.

Some of you will have found yourselves praying along with the characters. Some of you will have asked the Lord into your heart for the first time. Others will have prayed to more vigorously walk in faith by obeying what Jesus has told you to do. Others will have rededicated themselves to the Lord after a season of being slack in their walk with Him. Still others will find themselves repenting of attitudes and lifestyles they realize need to be changed.

Salvation is not a great mystery. If you have not yet prayed with the men and women of this book, but want to, do so now. You can do so alone.

You can do so with a friend, a parent, a pastor, a priest, a brother, a sister, a mentor. If a friend has given you this book, he or she would surely be glad to pray with you. You can pray aloud or in the quietness of your own heart.

Simply confess to God exactly what you feel. The words are not so important as that God knows your heart. If you speak to Him, and quiet yourself to listen, you will discover that He speaks in return. That's largely what being a Christian is all about—developing an inner dialogue with your Father, then doing what He tells you to do.

Most churches have studies and prayer groups where, in smaller and more intimate settings, men and women pray and grow together. Don't wait to be invited. Take the initiative. Go to church and inquire about such groups. Any pastor or priest will be happy to talk with you about your faith, especially if you are just starting out. Don't be afraid to ask questions.

Salvation as outlined here is not fundamentalist, liberal, Catholic, evangelical, Protestant, Episcopalian, charismatic or Lutheran. I have tried to set down a few of the components involved in being a "Christian"— which simply means a "follower of Christ." One can live out discipleship with Christ in *any* Christian church. Do not confuse the word *Christian* with a specific church or denominational label. The Bible is the guidebook for *all* of us together, and "salvation" is the doorway into the Christian faith for *all* Christian churches and denominations.

Once you have passed through the doorway into the life of the Christian faith and you want to make Jesus your Lord in a complete way, one of the most important elements for ongoing growth is to read the Gospels and do as instructed. This is the recipe for growth. Nothing is so vital to the development of the muscles of faith as learning the commands and instructions of Jesus and then *doing* what He said.

Michael Phillips

Books by Michael Phillips

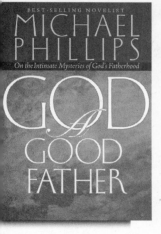

GOD A GOOD FATHER

In this startling book, Michael Phillips challenges the established Christian to step out of the status quo and into a breathtaking new relationship with God the Father. In a style reminiscent of John Bunyan's classic *Pilgrim's Progress*, Phillips acts as a "guide" on a journey to the place of the presence of our Heavenly Father.

A "divine restlessness" within you will be inspired as you follow Phillips out of the "fog-bound lowlands" of your typical existence and climb to the "mountain home of Abba Father," learning to know Him—His love, His goodness, His trustworthiness, His forgiveness—and choosing to live in His heart and drink of His water of life forever!

ISBN: 0-7684-2123-3

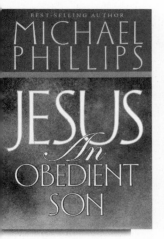

COMING IN THE FALL OF 2002

JESUS: AN OBEDIENT SON

He discovers a key that gives validity to an entire life's purpose and perspective as a Christian for right now. Not in some grandiose, far-reaching way…but the link between belief and practice, between eternity and now, between Christianity as a world religion and Christianity as a practical guidebook for going about the business of life in the trenches. For if ever a man walked in harmony between ultimate purpose and the next five minutes, that man was Jesus Christ. And that key to Jesus' life was obedience.

ISBN: 0-7684-2070-9

COMING IN THE WINTER OF 2003

KINGDOM CROSSING
ISBN: 0-7684-2152-7

Available at your local Christian bookstore.

For more information and sample chapters, visit www.destinyimage.com

Destiny Image Fiction
by Don Nori

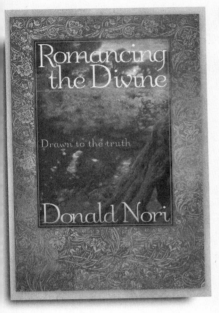

ROMANCING THE DIVINE

W ho among us experiences the fulfillment of divine love? How do we find the One our souls love? Does He love us equally in return? Here is a tale of every person's journey to find the reality of God. It is a tale of hope—a search for eternal love and for all the possibilities we have always imagined would be the conclusion of such a search. In this story you will most assuredly recognize your own search for God, and discover the divine fulfillment that His love brings.
ISBN: 0-7684-2053-9